lexile

TOFU

TLS

MYSTERIES IN OUR NATIONAL PARKS

MYSTERY
#9

MYSTERIES
IN OUR NATIONAL PARKS

ESCAPE FROM FEAR

GLORIA SKURZYNSKI AND ALANE FERGUSON

NATIONAL GEOGRAPHIC SOCIETY

WASHINGTON, D.C.

For Denise Georges,

who brought the island of St. John

to life for the authors

Text copyright © 2002 Gloria Skurzynski and Alane Ferguson
Cover illustration copyright © 2002 Loren Long

Map by Carl Mehler, Director of Maps
Map research and production by Matt Chwastyk
and Thomas L. Gray

Hawksbill turtle art by Joan Wolbier

This is a work of fiction. Any resemblance to living persons or events other than descriptions of natural phenomena is purely coincidental.

Library of Congress Cataloging-in-Publication Data

Skurzynski, Gloria.
  Escape from fear / by Gloria Skurzynski and Alane Ferguson.
    p. cm. — (Mysteries in our national parks ; #9)
Summary: While at St. John National Park in the Virgin Islands for a seminar on coral reefs, the Landons help a wealthy thirteen-year-old to find his birth mother, who he believes is in danger.
  ISBN 0-7922-6780-X (Hardcover)
  ISBN 0-7922-6782-6 (Paperback)
 [1. Racially mixed people--Fiction. 2. Adoption--Fiction. 3. Poaching--Fiction. 4. National parks and reserves. 5. Virgin Islands of the United States--Fiction. 6. Mystery and detective stories.] I. Ferguson, Alane. II. Title. III. Series.
  PZ7.S6287 Es 2002
  [Fic]--dc21
                                        2001005508

Printed in the United States of America

ACKNOWLEDGMENTS

The authors are very grateful to Ginger Garrison, Marine Ecologist, U.S. Geological Survey, and to the staff members of Virgin Islands National Park who so generously shared their expertise: Denise Georges, Park Ranger; Ken Wild, National Park Service archaeologist; Schuler Brown, Chief Ranger; Judy Shafer, Deputy Superintendent; and Rafe Boulon, Chief, Resource Management; and a special thanks to Miss Felicia, the basket-maker

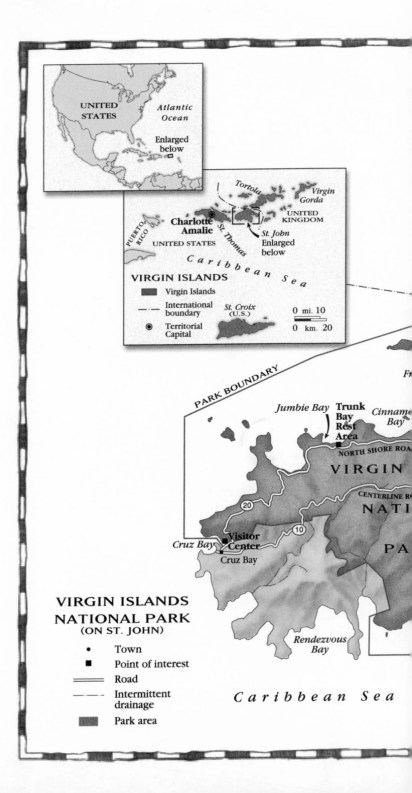

UNITED
STATES

*Atlantic
Ocean*

Enlarged
below

Tortola

*Virgin
Gorda*

**Charlotte
Amalie**

St. Thomas

UNITED
KINGDOM

St. John
Enlarged
below

PUERTO
RICO

UNITED STATES

C a r i b b e a n   S e a

VIRGIN ISLANDS

- ■ Virgin Islands
- ‒·‒ International boundary
- ⊙ Territorial Capital

St. Croix
(U.S.)

| 0 mi. 10 |
| 0 km. 20 |

PARK BOUNDARY

Fr

Jumbie Bay **Trunk
Bay
Rest
Area**

*Cinname
Bay*

NORTH SHORE ROA

VIRGIN

CENTERLINE R

NATI

20

10

Cruz Bay ■ **Visitor
Center**

PA

Cruz Bay

VIRGIN ISLANDS
NATIONAL PARK
(ON ST. JOHN)

- • Town
- ■ Point of interest
- ═══ Road
- ‒·‒ Intermittent drainage
- ▨ Park area

*Rendezvous
Bay*

C a r i b b e a n   S e a

PARK DATA

Territory: St. John, U.S. Virgin Islands

Established: 1956

Area: 12,909 acres, including 5,650 acres underwater

Climate: Average year-round temperature is 79°F; average annual rainfall is more than 40 inches, with most precipitation occurring in spring (mainly April and May) and fall (September to November)

Natural Features: Crystal clear, turquoise bays; white sand beaches; coral reefs; mangrove habitats; and the best examples of dry tropical forest in the Caribbean

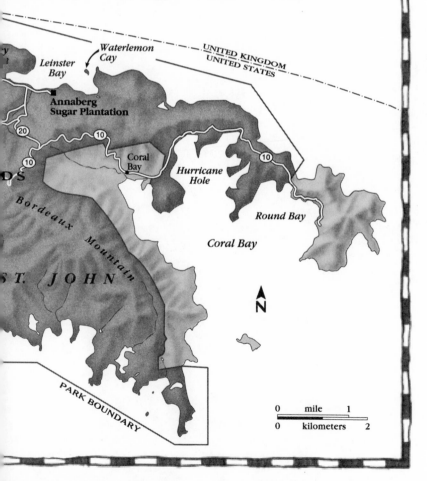

The beach stretched in front of him, a gleaming sweep of moonlit whiteness edged by a thick stand of trees. A perfect spot, the man told himself—secluded, wild, and most important of all, a place where there would be no witnesses.

It was when he'd dropped anchor into the ink-black water that he saw her, alone and vulnerable. Her eyes, large in the moonlight, watched him silently. She knew he was there.

"You see that?" he asked his accomplice, steadying himself as a wave broke against the bow. It sprayed a fine mist that glittered in the moonlight.

"I see dat. She be good, mon. So we goes an' catch dis one big beautiful t'ing."

Yes, they would take her. More money would fatten his wallet thanks to this lucky find. She was icing on his cake. Slipping into the waves, he made his way toward her....

CHAPTER ONE

Jack looked down, straining to catch a glimpse of ocean beneath him, but all he could see were endless white clouds floating like enormous swirls of meringue. After three hours in the air—just on this leg of the trip—he was more than anxious to reach his destination, Virgin Islands National Park on the island of St. John. He'd been dreaming of white beaches and turquoise waters, where rainbow-colored fish swam as thick as snowflakes and the water was as warm as the sunshine. After an icy Wyoming winter, he was ready for instant summer. Besides, with his skin the color of a fish's underbelly, he needed to get started on a tan.

"Jack, where's your sister?" his mother asked from a seat directly behind him.

"Looking for a *People* magazine," Jack answered. "She's trying to mooch one out of First Class."

"You know she's not supposed to go in there—if they catch her they'll toss her right back into Coach." A beat later, she asked, "Don't you think she's been gone an awfully long time?"

Jack shrugged. "Mom, we're on an airplane. Even Ashley can't get lost on an airplane."

His mother, Olivia, was small—already shorter than Jack, who, at 13, stood at almost five feet seven inches. Olivia's dark curly hair had been pulled into a ponytail, and she wore no makeup except lip gloss. Jack could see a three-inch stack of papers on her folding tray, marked with red lines and exclamation points that made the paper look as though it were bleeding red ink. Since they'd left Jackson Hole, she'd been poring though publications about coral reefs and hawksbill turtles, scratching notes in the margins of books and rereading research papers. National Parks frequently called Olivia, a wildlife veterinarian, for help when a species became threatened. The case in St. John involved a larger problem—Earth's coral reefs were dying at an alarming rate. Since much of Virgin Islands National Park on St. John lay underwater, reef loss was hurting many species, including the endangered hawksbill turtles.

"Steven, don't you think Ashley's been gone too long?" Olivia prodded. "It's been half an hour."

Next to Olivia sat Jack's dad, Steven, his reading glasses perched on the end of his thin nose. Steven, a professional photographer, had immersed himself in the newest photography magazine. Jack could see the beginning of a bald spot in the overhead light that cast a small circle on the top of his father's blond head. "She's probably busy chatting with the flight attendants," Steven murmured without looking up.

Olivia scanned the aisle. "Maybe you're right. I swear, that child has never met a stranger."

"Which is why she's been so good with our foster kids." Pulling off his glasses, Steven dropped them into his shirt pocket and said, "You know, I was just thinking how long it's been since we've had a trip with just the four of us. It seems we've had a foster kid or two to stir things up on every single park visit. What are we going to do without all the excitement?"

"Rest. Play. Relax!" Jack broke in. At least, that was what he was counting on. What his dad said was true—every single time the Landons had been scheduled to leave on a trip, it seemed, a foster kid materialized at almost the last second. But not this trip. Now it was just his own family on the way to paradise, exactly the way Jack wanted it. Settling back into his seat, he heard his mother murmur something he couldn't quite make out, to which his father replied, "OK, if it will make you feel better, I'll go find her."

"You don't need to, Dad," Jack said, pointing. "There she is. Check it out—Ashley's coming from First Class. And it looks like she's bringing a friend."

His sister's small frame seemed to bounce with every step as she made her way down the narrow aisle. Behind her was a boy close to Jack's age, as perfectly pressed as an airline pilot—tan khakis, the kind with a knife pleat down the front, topped by an impeccably tailored navy-blue blazer worn over a red-and-white cotton shirt. Whoever this guy was, it looked as though he definitely did not want to trail after Ashley through Coach. Poor sucker, Jack thought. He wasn't the first to be pulled into Ashley's tractor beam.

"Hey, Jack, Mom, Dad, say 'hi' to Forrest," Ashley urged, presenting Forrest with a wave of her hand. "I practically dragged him back here, but I told him he just *had* to come and meet you all."

"How do you do, Mr. and Dr. Landon," Forrest said, giving a slight bow. "Hello, Jack. Your sister has told me a lot about you."

"Yeah, I can imagine," Jack muttered.

Tall and thin, Forrest had skin the color of mocha ice cream. Dark, close-cropped hair wreathed his scalp in tight curls. His lips were full, his nose wide and strong, but Jack noticed something else about him: When he spoke, Forrest's dark, almond eyes never quite met Jack's, as if he were looking just the barest degree beyond Jack's head. Strange, Jack thought.

"You're not going to believe how I met him!" Ashley announced. "We've been talking the whole time I've been gone." A smaller version of Olivia, Ashley had the same mass of ringlets, totally opposite of the straight, yellow hair Jack had inherited from his father. "There was a *People* magazine on an empty seat next to him in First Class," she went on, "and I asked if he was reading it and he said 'no' and we started talking and I told him about you, Mom, and your hawksbill turtles missing from the coral reefs and then the flight attendant came and she said I had to leave but Forrest told her I was a friend of his and I could stay if he said so. He made her bring me a Coke and she put it in a real glass, not in a plastic cup like we get in Coach. The seats in First Class are enormous—it's like they have their own sofa! And you know what else?"

"Don't worry, she's always like this," Jack interjected. "Ashley doesn't have an 'off' button. But we keep looking for one." He started to smile, but decided not to when he saw Forrest's unamused expression.

"Very funny, Jack. Ha, ha," Ashley said. Dropping into her seat, she hardly missed a breath. "What I was *going* to say before I was so *rudely* interrupted was that Forrest's dad is a United States diplomat. Forrest something-something. What is it again?" She looked at Forrest expectantly.

Hesitating, the boy said, "Forrest Winthrop III."

"Right. Which makes you Forrest Winthrop IV, right?"

"Your father's a diplomat?" Olivia asked. "Hmm, very impressive. I'd like to meet him."

"That's just it, Mom," Ashley rushed in. "His dad's

not here. Or his mom. Forrest is flying all by himself. He's only 13, and he came all the way from Denver through two different airports—he's been traveling over 12 hours already."

Surprised, Jack said, "Twelve hours by yourself? Man, that's a lot of flying."

"I've been negotiating airports all my life," Forrest answered indifferently.

It was hard to believe that he and Forrest were the same age. Sitting up taller, Jack squared his shoulders, hoping it made him look more mature. Just then a woman with a baby came up behind Forrest, waiting for the aisle to clear. She looked at him impatiently. In one fluid motion, Forrest stepped aside and signaled her to walk on, his movement as graceful as a dancer's. Then, clasping his hands behind his back, he turned his attention back to the Landons. For some reason, Jack felt irritated. He tried to push the feeling down and keep his own face blank.

Steven asked, "Are your parents going to meet you in St. Thomas, Forrest?"

"No." Hesitating, he said, "My…cousins."

"Your cousins are coming to the airport?"

"Yes."

"If you'd like us to wait to make sure they arrive—"

"Thank you, but that won't be necessary." It was then that Jack saw a change in Forrest's face, a new expression pulled into place like a mask. A perfect smile flashed across perfect white teeth, as though it had been rehearsed a thousand times, but there was something the smile didn't quite cover. Jack wondered if Steven and Olivia saw it, too.

Glancing at what looked to be a very expensive watch, Forrest said, "Well, Ashley, I'm glad you talked me into meeting your family, but I'd better get back to my seat. We should be making our final descent soon." He held out his hand to Steven. "Mr. Landon, it was a pleasure to meet you." And to Olivia, "Dr. Landon, I wish you luck with your turtles. Jack, enjoy your trip, and Ashley, come to First Class anytime. Good-bye."

"Bye," Ashley said, giving a tiny wave. "Thanks again for the Coke."

Like the wizard in Oz, Forrest disappeared behind the curtain into First Class.

"Isn't he something?" Ashley asked, eyes wide. "The way he talks it's like he's 30 years old. He goes to a private school. And he's on the soccer team."

Steven nodded. "Yes, he's very impressive. I'm surprised his parents let him go it alone like that, but he seems to be doing fine. So, Ashley, you managed to weasel a Coke out of him, did you?" Steven chuckled. "Figures. I'm amazed you didn't finagle a whole meal."

"Forrest asked if I wanted one, but I said I wasn't hungry. He must have piles of money. You know, we've had lots of kids staying with us, but I've never met anyone like Forrest."

"The very rich are different from you and me," Olivia said without looking up from her reading. "F. Scott Fitzgerald said that. I think he's right."

Steven rubbed his chin, thoughtful. "Maybe not. When all is said and done, Forrest's still a child. I want to keep an eye on him and make sure he hooks up with his cousins when we land. The airport is no place for a kid, no matter how rich he is."

Jack pressed his head against the window and looked into the darkening sky. Typical, he thought. His parents had always held out their hands to anyone who needed help. Fortunately, Forrest looked as though he was managing fine on his own. That was good. There was something about that guy Jack didn't like, something he couldn't quite put his finger on. Well, it didn't make any difference. They'd land at the airport and go their separate ways, and that would be the end of it.

The sun was setting in a ball of fire, turning the night sky ablaze. As they made their descent, the sun disappeared completely, sending the plane into a velvet darkness.

"I see lights. Is that St. Thomas?" Ashley asked, leaning across Jack to press her face against his window.

"I think so. Wow, look at all those lights—it's like the island is on fire. A lot of people must live there!" St. Thomas, one of the U.S. Virgin Islands, was not the Landons' final destination, but it was the island with the nearest airport. They'd take a ferry to St. John.

"I can't believe we're almost here!" Ashley exclaimed. "First thing tomorrow I want to go snorkeling and stay in the water until night."

"If you do, you'll wrinkle up like a raisin," Jack told her. "Remember Hawaii? Mom said we were going to have to iron you back to normal."

"So?" Ashley retorted. "It was worth it. I wonder if Forrest is going to snorkel."

"If he does he won't wrinkle. He's w-a-a-y too starched for that."

Punching him in the arm, Ashley said, "I thought he was nice!"

"Yeah, whatever." Before she could say anything more, Jack exclaimed, "Look, we're about to touch down. Three…two…one!"

They landed with a gentle bump, the engines screaming as the plane came to a stop. Everyone spilled out of their seats, popping open overhead bins and crowding into the aisle until no one moved at all. No one, Jack realized, except those in First Class, who got to leave the plane ahead of everyone else. The rest of the passengers, weary from the long flight, had to wait before they slowly filed off the plane.

Once outside, the first thing Jack noticed was the humidity. It enfolded him like a wet blanket, thick and heavy with smoky airplane fuel that mingled with the honeyed scent of island flowers. Lights blazed overhead, so bright that Jack cast a shadow as he made his way inside the small, crowded terminal. His attention was immediately caught by some men in cotton shirts and pants of wildly colored prints, wearing hats that sat high on their heads.

"Rastifarians," his mother explained. "They don't ever cut their hair. They tuck it up into those hats."

Through the milling people, Jack spotted Forrest at an information desk. He looked at Jack, then turned away quickly, as though Jack were now a complete stranger. The woman behind the counter handed a map to Forrest and pointed to a main exit.

"Are you noticing Forrest?" Steven asked Olivia.

"Yes, I'm noticing. There's no one here to meet him."

"I wonder where his cousins are."

The carousel turned slowly, churning out bag after bag like a giant Pez dispenser. Jack grabbed his and Ashley's, while Steven pulled out the one he and Olivia shared. Jack noticed his father's eyes were still locked on Forrest, who was handing the woman a credit card.

"Come on, Dad, don't worry about Forrest," Jack pleaded. "He'll be fine."

"I'm sure you're right," Steven answered, his hand resting lightly on Jack's shoulder. "But I think I'll go talk to him, just to be sure."

Too late. Quickly, efficiently, Forrest slipped his wallet into his pants pocket and glided out the door, disappearing into the night, all alone.

CHAPTER TWO

"He's gone now," Steven sighed. "Obviously, he was lying to us on the plane. Forrest's traveling by himself, which is a very dangerous thing for a child to do."

"You don't know that he's alone, Steven," Olivia replied. "Maybe his cousins' plans changed suddenly."

Steven shook his head. "There's something going on with that kid—I can feel it. I just wish I knew what it was." He stared at the colorful crowd before adding, "Well, there's nothing we can do for him now. Jack, give me a hand with the bags. We've got to find a taxi to take us to the dock."

Jack didn't want to admit how relieved he felt that Forrest was gone from their lives, so he kept his eyes on the bags as he wheeled them to the front doors. The taxi turned out to be a big van that seated ten people and their mound of luggage. Since he got to sit up front next to the driver, he had the best view of the streets of St. Thomas. Lights shone from houses perched upon the surrounding hills. Narrow roads switchbacked in breathtaking turns. More than once, Jack had to close his eyes as the driver careened around sharp corners; when he looked back, he noticed his mother gripping the edge of her seat.

"Are we going to die?" Ashley whispered.

"I'm sure the driver is in complete control," Olivia answered, trying to convince herself as much as Ashley.

Finally, the taxi screeched to a halt and everyone spilled out onto the dock. Boys not much older than Jack leaped forward to carry the luggage to the white, two-tiered ferryboat that bobbed on gentle waves.

"Can we sit up on the top deck?" Ashley begged.

"Absolutely," Steven told her. "Go on and lead the way." Since the upper deck was uncrowded, each of the Landons got a bench, one behind the other. They hung their arms over the rail so they could peer into the ebony water 20 feet below. On impulse, Jack got up from his bench and went to sit next to his father.

"It's pretty spectacular, isn't it," Steven said, smiling. "See those lights? Seems like someone's having a party."

Jack looked at what he guessed was a restaurant. The wooden building had been decorated with white lights that reflected against the water in ropes of stars.

"You know, I saw a lot of young people going in that direction. I wonder if Forrest will end up there?"

Shrugging in reply, Jack hoped his irritation didn't show. He must have failed at hiding it because a moment later his father asked, "Is something wrong, son?"

"No."

"Then why do you have that look on your face?"

"What look?"

"The one where your forehead wrinkles up and you scowl. The one you've got right now."

Jack made a real effort to smooth his expression. "It's…I guess I don't know why you're so worried about Forrest all of a sudden. I mean, why do you even care?" His words came out in a rush. "It's just—I don't want an extra kid with us, Dad. We always take foster kids along on our trips, but this time it's just our family, and I want to keep it that way. It's not like the social workers assigned him to us or anything. We're not responsible. If he's run away or he's off on his own, I don't see why that's any of our business. Is it?"

Just then the ferry got underway, stirring a breeze that quickly turned into a rush of wind. Ashley's hair blew out in dark ribbons while Jack's jacket ballooned around his chest. Air that had felt so warm moments before now chilled him. He watched as his mother pulled her collar close around her neck.

As far back as Jack could remember, his mother had taken care of animals or anything that was hurt, and that extended to neighbors and friends and stray children. He was glad she hadn't heard what he'd just said to his father; she would probably tell him he was acting selfish. Well, for once he didn't care. Why couldn't some other family step in for a change? He'd almost decided his father wasn't going to answer his question when Steven said, "Jack, I told you about the time I ran away, didn't I?"

"Yeah, when you headed off to Idaho. You were in a bad foster home, right? I forget how old you were—"

"Twelve. Hardly big enough to lick a stamp and there I was, hitching a ride west with the aim of trying my hand at farmwork." He looked off into the distance. "It was a stupid thing to do—a risky thing. I don't know what would have happened if Carlos hadn't taken me under his wing and talked me into going back. Do you understand what I'm saying?"

Jack wasn't sure, but he said, "I guess so."

"Things could have been very different if that migrant worker hadn't stepped in and helped me out. There was nothing in it for Carlos, nothing but the good that comes from helping a fellow human being. Carlos taught me a lot—things I don't want to forget."

Jack couldn't help thinking that the situation with Forrest was completely different from his dad's, but he decided to drop the conversation, and his father didn't press. Minutes passed in silence as the prow of the ferry cut through the water. Jack knew there were other islands nearby, but all he could see was the little white-capped waves and all he could hear was the engine sounds that lulled him. When his eyes closed—just for a minute—pictures of his father flashed through his mind: His dad hitching a ride in a red pickup, Steven walking through a potato field, and, oddly, his dad as a kid talking to Forrest about a storm that was coming in from the west, a bad storm that could kill them all. Jack could feel his head rock on his shoulders as he fought the heaviness of sleep, and then he felt his father's arm, warm and strong, encircle him before he gave in to his dream.

"We're here. Wake up, Jack."

Jack's eyes flew open as he realized they must have arrived at St. John. His mother stood over him, gently shaking his shoulder. Ashley was already leaning over the railing, her hair wind-whipped to three times its normal size, chattering to Steven as they watched people from the lower deck stream onto the dock.

"Hey, are you finally awake?" Ashley asked when he stumbled over to where she stood. "You sure were out of it. You were drooling like a St. Bernard."

"Yeah, well, you look like you've got a tumbleweed stuck on your head," Jack replied, yawning. He stretched hard, pushing the blood back into his limbs.

With both hands, Ashley tried to mash down her wild hair. She was about to say something more when her eyes widened. Pointing to where the last of the lower deck passengers stepped off the gangplank, she cried, "Look—oh my gosh—it's Forrest! He must have been on the bottom deck of the ferry the whole time. We didn't even see him! Mom, Dad, there he is!"

With cool confidence Forrest walked to where the luggage had been piled and picked up his bag, slinging it over his shoulder. Again there was no one to meet him, and he obviously was not looking for anyone. He'd come to St. John all by himself.

"He's still alone," Olivia said, her voice grim. "Steven, what should we do?"

"What do you think, Jack?"

Jack shifted uncomfortably under his father's gaze, which seemed to pin him right into the wooden deck. He knew what he should say, so he made himself say it. "I guess we'd better go talk to him."

Ashley cried, "He's leaving!"

"OK, everyone, move fast," Steven ordered.

The four of them clambered down the steps onto the wooden dock. Again young boys crowded forward, offering to carry their luggage, this time to waiting taxis that looked like ice-cream trucks with colored canopies, but the Landons rushed past. Steven reached Forrest first, clapping his hand onto the boy's shoulder while the rest of the Landons hurried to catch up. When Forrest whipped around, he seemed visibly dismayed.

"Oh...hello...Mr. Landon," he stammered.

Steven sounded pleasant enough, but Jack could tell he was on edge. "I'm surprised to see you in St. John. I thought you said you were going to St. Thomas."

"I…changed my mind."

"Where are your cousins?"

"They're around here, somewhere," Forrest said, shaking his shoulder free. He crossed his arms, as if daring Steven to ask him more questions.

"I'd like to meet them."

"*No!* I mean, thank you for your concern." Jack noticed a bead of perspiration roll down the edge of Forrest's face. He must be wilting in the moist evening heat. Or maybe he was more nervous than he was letting on. "Look, Mr. Landon, I don't want to be rude, but what I do really isn't any of your business."

"I'm afraid it is," Steven answered quietly. "I was just talking to Jack about that. You're only 13 years old, you're thousands of miles from home, and you're here all alone. That makes it my business."

"And mine," Olivia agreed, edging closer to Steven.

Jack could tell that Forrest was going to bolt. His arms, his whole body tensed, and in one quick motion he tried to escape, but Steven grabbed him and hung on. "Whoa, take it easy. We're only trying to help you."

"I don't want your help. I don't *need* it! Let me *go!*" Forrest demanded. He pulled furiously, but it was useless. Steven had him tight.

"Just tell me—have you run away?"

"None of your business!" Forrest spat.

"OK, then at least tell me where you plan to stay. You can share that much, can't you?" Steven's voice had regained its steady calm. "If you tell me what your plans are, then I'm sure it will all work out."

Raising his head proudly, Forrest declared, "I have money. I'll get a hotel room with my platinum card."

"For heaven's sake, is that what you were planning to do? You can't get a room at the spur of the moment on St. John, not this time of year," Olivia retorted. "There are no hotel rooms." When he looked at her blankly, she said, "It's spring break, Forrest. The island is overflowing with vacationing college students right now. You can't even rent a closet."

This seemed to startle him, and the last bit of smugness faded from his face. Olivia shot a glance toward Steven. After his nod of approval, she said, "You're going to need a place to stay tonight, and you can't stay on the beach. You'd better come with us."

Forrest's chin jutted out again. "What if I say no?"

"We're not going to leave you on your own. We'll take you to the police and let them deal with you," Steven answered. "Is that how you want to play this?"

Most of the other people from the ferry had already driven away on the ice-cream truck taxis, but one lone truck drove up to where Jack and his family were standing. "Lady, you want taxi?" a man in a striped linen shirt asked. His face was a shining tan, and his hat looked as though it had been planted on the back of his head. "I help wid dis luggage," he said. "Where do I take you?"

"Well," Olivia asked Forrest, "what's it going to be?"

"Just come with us. Please?" Ashley pleaded.

Jack said nothing. He watched Forrest sag, just a little, before he finally gave in. "All right. I accept. Thank you. Please…please, don't ask me why I've done what I've done. I have my reasons. That's all I want to say."

"There'll be plenty of time to sort out the 'why's' in the morning," Steven told him. "That much can wait. But we will be calling your parents as soon as we get to our motel. They must be worried sick."

Forrest did not reply. Woodenly, he got into the cab and pushed himself into the farthest corner. Ashley followed, then Jack, and then his parents, crammed in so close their knees touched.

"Here we go," the man called out as his truck-cab rumbled to life. Though almost eleven at night, the streets were full of partying students from the U.S. mainland, mingling with island natives as they danced to music blaring from open-fronted, neon-lit restaurants. On the sidewalks, shorts-clad senior citizens walked hand in hand while neon lights reflected on their faces. Ashley tried to coax Forrest to speak, but he kept his head down as the taxi bumped along the uneven streets.

Their cab driver beeped his horn to warn people out of the way. The air felt warm and sweet with the scent of flowers they could barely see in the darkness; the crowds seemed happy and full of high spirits. St. John appeared to have no intention of quieting down for the night. Jack would have been feeling pretty high himself, except for the knot in his stomach. They were stuck with an extra kid, exactly the way he knew it would happen. Well, they couldn't keep Forrest too long. They'd probably turn him over to some authority in the morning. He tried to remember what his father had said about Carlos. So far, it wasn't working.

In minutes, the taxi stopped in front of a cast-iron gate that guarded a courtyard in the center of several darkened buildings. "You guys get the luggage while I find someone to check us in," Olivia told them. "Forrest, as soon as we find our rooms, Steven and I will call your parents."

Forrest nodded.

They'd booked two rooms, which would work out OK since it seemed that Forrest would be spending the night with them. He and Jack could stay in one room while Ashley slept on a cot in her parents' room. They often divided up motel rooms that way, if the foster child happened to be a boy. Jack knew the drill.

They bumped the suitcases up a flight of narrow concrete stairs, waiting for Olivia to arrive with the room keys. She opened one door, then the one next to it. That's when Jack saw where he'd be staying.

A ten-foot-square room with sagging twin beds greeted him. One small Formica end table held one lamp with a moth batting against the bulb. The cinder-block walls had been painted a lifeless tan. The floor's pattern had been walked off long ago.

Looking surprised and a bit grim, Steven surveyed the room, but all he said was, "Well, it's not paradise, but it's all we could get. Where's the telephone?"

"I don't know," Jack answered. "First let me get some air going, Dad. It's like an oven in here." Jack turned on the window fan, but it only stirred a small, hot breeze. After he jumped up to pull a chain dangling from a ceiling fan, the overhead fan blades started to rotate slowly, pushing hot waves around the room. What a dump, Jack thought.

"Maybe the phone's in the bathroom," Ashley suggested, pushing open the door to the tiny room. It had a stand-up shower stall, no tub, and towels about as thick as handkerchiefs.

"There's not even a phone, and I'm supposed to stay here?" Forrest blurted in disbelief.

"Bet it's better than jail," Jack retorted. "Or on the beach. Which is where you'd have been."

"Jack," his mother said firmly, a signal for Jack to back off. "Steven, I noticed a pay phone in a booth in the courtyard. I guess we'll have to use that. Forrest, give me your parents' phone number."

Forrest pulled a monogrammed leather wallet from an inside pocket of his navy-blue blazer, which he still wore buttoned up in spite of the heat in the room. "Here it is on the back of my dad's card. This is the number of the embassy in Paris."

Steven took the thick, cream-colored business card

and stared at it. "Forrest Winthrop III," he read.

"Right. As I told you, I'm Forrest Winthrop IV." The words sounded grim. "Mr. Landon, is calling them in the middle of the night absolutely necessary?"

Steven took a deep breath, and Jack knew he was thinking hard about waiting. In the end, he said, "Running away is a serious thing, and your parents have a right to know where you are. I think you should come with me so you can tell them yourself."

"I'm sorry, but I can't. If you give me the phone, I won't speak to them."

Jack heard his father say something that sounded like "I'm too old for this," but he wasn't sure. "Anyone know what time it is right now in Paris?" Steven asked. "Four in the morning? Five?" When his family shook their heads no, Steven sighed. "You probably know, don't you, Forrest?"

Forrest shrugged.

"Well, I guess I'll have to call the operator and ask. Forrest, is there a message—a reason—you'd like me to give your parents?"

"No."

"Then what should I tell them when they ask why you ran away?"

"Tell them...," he said, hesitating, "...that I wasn't running away. I was running 'to.' Tell them *I know*. I'm sure they'll understand."

CHAPTER THREE

Erb *er erb er eeeerrrr!*

The noise pierced Jack's brain like a jolt of electricity. In a flash Forrest was up, peering out his window. Through half opened eyes, Jack could see the sky had lightened to the color of silver as morning broke across the horizon of St. John. Forrest, in shorts and T-shirt, craned to glimpse the source of the noise.

Erb er erb er eeeerrrr!

"Man, what *is* that?" Forrest asked.

"Go back to bed," Jack moaned. "It's just a rooster."

"A rooster? What's a rooster doing outside our hotel?"

Jack yawned a gaping yawn and flung an arm over his eyes. "We're in a *motel,* not a *hotel,* remember? Haven't you ever heard a rooster crow before?"

"There aren't many animals in our dorm—unless you count the juniors and seniors," Forrest snickered.

When the rooster crowed again, Jack wrapped his pillow firmly around his ears. "It's 5 a.m.," he groaned. "My body clock says it's two o'clock. Go to sleep."

Although Forrest kept muttering beneath his breath, Jack could make out every word. "My soccer league has stayed in plenty of bottom-of-the-barrel hotels, but I've never had to endure a dump like this."

"Quit whining," Jack retorted. "That's all you've done since we found you."

"I'm not whining, I'm commenting."

"Then quit commenting and go to sleep."

Forrest slipped beneath the thin cotton sheet. Bed springs groaned as he turned on his right side, flipped to his left, then back to his right once more. Jack was just drifting off when Forrest's husky whisper pulled him back. "Jack?"

"Hmmmm?"

There was a pause, then a muffled, "Never mind."

Closing his eyes, Jack tried to ignore Forrest, but he couldn't shake the feeling that he was being watched in the room's half-light. Forrest kept staring, watching, waiting. Jack's parents would want him to try to draw Forrest out since he wouldn't tell them anything more about his cryptic message. Running *to?* they'd asked. What did *that* mean? But even Ashley hadn't been able to get him to talk. And now, in the middle of the night, Forrest seemed to want to chat. Figured. Pulling the pillow off his face, Jack sighed. "OK. What?"

"Do you…do you think your parents will keep me? Or will they turn me over to the authorities?"

"I don't know," Jack answered. "Why couldn't you ask me all this before we went to bed?"

"I didn't feel like talking then. I do now. So what do you think?"

"It depends on what *your* parents decide. Since my dad couldn't get through to them at the embassy last night, we don't know anything for sure."

"The embassy will open soon. I know my parents, and they'll let me stay with your family until they come to retrieve me. But the question is, will your folks go through the hassle of keeping me till then?" He paused and added, "I really need to know."

And I really need to sleep, but you don't care, do you, Jack groaned inwardly. Pale daylight sliced through the cheap curtains, creating a lattice work of shadows on the walls. Jack raised up on his elbow and faced Forrest's outline. "We take in kids all the time. My folks are registered as temporary-care foster parents." With a sinking feeling, he put into words what he'd hoped wouldn't be true. "I bet you'll stay."

"Good!" Forrest sighed. "That's good. I *can't* be locked up. It would ruin everything."

"Ruin what? Are you going to talk in riddles again? Why don't you just tell me what's going on?"

Forrest didn't answer, but Jack could see him shaking his head.

"Are you worried about what's going to happen when your folks find out you've run off? I mean, are you going to be grounded for life or something?" He figured Forrest would get in major, spectacular trouble for taking off on an airplane and making his parents fly after him all the way from Paris. If Jack ever pulled a stunt like that, his mom and dad would lock him up and throw away the key.

"Grounded?" Forrest snorted. "I've never been grounded in my life. No, I'm not worried about that. I know how to handle adults."

That arrogant response irritated Jack, so he said, "You mean your parents won't even care?"

"Of course they'll care—my father will be livid. My mother will probably just cry and tell me how much I've disappointed her. But you know what? *They've* disappointed *me*. Look at my skin!" he cried, jutting out his arm as if Jack could discern something important in the dimness. "They always told me it didn't matter that I was half black because I was their *chosen* son. They said I had no past, only a future. I used to believe them. But they don't know what I found out...." His voice broke off suddenly. Jack waited as Forrest lay on his bed, unmoving, mute.

Jack pushed himself into a sitting position. The thin sheet draped like a tent between his knees as he tried to think how to keep Forrest talking, because all this evasiveness was making Jack more and more curious.

"So…you won't get into much trouble when they come and get you, right? You're lucky."

"It's not 'they'—it's 'she.' My father will send my mother. She does his errands. He's an important diplomat, remember?" Forrest let out a loud sigh. "Look, the fact is, I can't afford to trust you or anyone. I don't even know you—you're just somebody I met on the plane." Rolling over, he clutched his covers and pulled them over his chest. "Just forget this whole conversation."

"Wait a minute—back up. Saying you can't trust me," Jack sputtered, "that's an insult."

"No. I can't reveal anything. It could be dangerous."

"How? Are you guarding some kind of nuclear secret or something and the spies are trying to snag you and if you tell me they'll have to kill us both?" Jack made it sound as ridiculous as possible.

"The less you know, the better."

Even though it was too dim for Forrest to see, Jack rolled his eyes. There was no way he was going to believe that a guy like Forrest, with his preppy manners and perfect clothes, could be involved in something dangerous. Sure, Forrest had enough spare cash in his account to hop on a plane—*First Class*—and come to St. John, which meant he lived a very different life. Jack could believe "different." But to be involved in something *dangerous?* He wondered if Forrest IV had a clue how absurd he sounded. He didn't even *talk* like a kid—more like some snooty college professor. "OK, don't tell *me* if you don't want to," Jack said, frustrated, "but I know my parents would try to help you—"

"Do not repeat anything I told you, understand?" Forrest's voice chilled as he put a space between each word. "I mean it, Jack. I may have said too much—OK, that's my fault. But I expect you to keep your mouth shut. Unless you're a squealer." He paused. "Are you?"

For a moment, the question hung in the air. Finally, Jack whispered, "No."

"I didn't think so." With his back toward Jack, Forrest clutched his pillow and thumped it hard. "Now if you'll excuse me, I'm going to try to get some more sleep."

"Hey—maybe this time I won't let *you* sleep."

Silence.

"I'll shut up if you tell me about this big secret you're carrying around."

More silence. Jack watched as Forrest's sides rose and fell in sudden, rhythmic breathing. He wasn't asleep—no one could nod off in seconds like that. But it let Jack know he'd been dismissed. As far as Forrest was concerned, the conversation was over.

Sliding back down onto his hot mattress, Jack kept his eyes focused on the slowly whirling ceiling fan overhead, forcing his mind onto other things—good things—like snorkeling in the bays around St. John. He made a mental checklist of the supplies he'd need: Film, check; camera lenses and filters, check; sunscreen, check. Without that, Jack—unlike Forrest whose skin was naturally dark—would broil like a lobster. Forrest, the guy with the big mystery. What could he be running *to?*

The question dimmed in Jack's mind as he drifted back to sleep, dreaming of Forrest IV being chased into the Caribbean Sea by an enormous, crowing rooster.

#

Knocking reverberated through the room. Jack heard the door open and close, and then his father's voice said, "Time to get up. Your mother has a meeting at Park Headquarters. Forrest, good for you."

Forrest, good for you—what did that mean? Jack struggled to open his eyes. The clock next to him read 8:00. Forrest stood there, already dressed, looking as pressed and as perfect as he had on the plane, his shampooed hair still damp and curling in tight ringlets. "Good morning, Mr. Landon," he said. "Were you able to get in touch with my parents this morning?"

"I tried to contact the embassy again, but I'm having a lot of trouble getting an international line on that pay phone down in the courtyard."

Since Steven had left the door wide open, the sounds and smells of St. John tumbled inside: The low rumble of trucks, the chattering of birds, the air tinged with lemon. As Jack swung his legs over the side of the bed, he rubbed his belly sleepily.

"Forrest and I will meet you in the courtyard. Move it, son. We need to plan our day."

CHAPTER FOUR

Steven and Olivia, Ashley and Forrest were seated at a white plastic table. Ashley waved when she saw Jack and then took a bite out of a slice of cantaloupe. A fountain bubbled nearby, its surface littered with brown flower petals. From behind a counter a waitress emerged. Carrying a large tray laden with fruit and coffee mugs, she wove her way between the eight other tables. Jack slipped into a plastic chair and said, "Hey, Forrest, thanks for leaving me a towel."

"Weren't there any more? I'll need to tell the maid to bring an extra set for this afternoon. I always like to take a second shower when it's hot like this."

"I can go to the front desk and get extras, Forrest," Ashley volunteered.

"Forrest can get his own towels," Jack grumbled.

Setting down a piece of lemon bread, Steven stared

at Jack. "Did you sleep all right, son?" he asked. Jack knew what the question really meant. It translated into, 'Why are you so cranky?'"

"Uh—I'm kind of tired. Forrest woke me up when it was still dark, and then we started talking."

"Talking?" Olivia looked at Forrest expectantly."

Forrest shot Jack a look, which Jack returned straight on. No, he wouldn't say anything about their conversation—what was there to tell, anyway? Now that the sun was beating down on the top of his head, warming a spot on his scalp, everything Forrest had said about dangerous secrets seemed nothing more than a dream-like, middle-of-the-night fantasy.

"He just woke up because of that stupid rooster, that's all," Jack told them.

Relieved, Forrest slid some butter on his poppy-seed muffin and took a careful bite, making sure no crumbs fell on his Tommy Hilfiger knit shirt.

"Well, he's remaining mysterious with us, too," Olivia said. "We can't seem to get a straight answer out of him. I was hoping he'd explain everything this morning, but he's not cooperating. Are you, Forrest?"

"I already told you, I have my reasons."

"Mmm." Olivia didn't sound convinced. "Well, the first and biggest problem we've got right now is contacting his parents. We can't seem to get through to the embassy on that pay phone—it keeps disconnecting us. So here's the plan. I've already called Park Headquarters and explained what's happened, and they offered the use of their phones. Your dad needs to stay with me at headquarters so he can track down Forrest's parents while I'm in my meeting."

"Wait a minute—Dad's taking us snorkeling!" Jack protested, but Olivia held up her hand, cutting him off.

"I know, I know, but things have changed. Luckily for you, the park has an interpretative ranger named Denise Georges who volunteered to help us out. She said she'd take you kids around the island while I'm in my meeting and your dad is making arrangements for Forrest. We'll reconvene at two o'clock."

"But, Mom, I've already got everything packed for snorkeling! So does Ashley!"

"I realize that, but right now we have to compromise." She looked directly at Jack. "Understand?"

"I'm sorry to put you out like this," Forrest apologized. "Another option would be for you to let me leave now. You were right last night—I really was unprepared for some of the—" he seemed to choose his word carefully—"*details* in spending the night here. But surely there's *one* room on the island that I can book. Let me find that room, and I'll stay there. I promise I'll call my parents and tell them everything, and then I can get on with my business, and you can get on with yours."

"Not a chance," Steven told him firmly.

"But there are things I need to do here!"

"Can you tell us about it?" Olivia asked. "We'd like

to help you, if we could. Tell us what it is you're running to. What is it your parents will 'understand'?"

Forrest shook his head. He kept his eyes on his napkin, rubbing his fingertips against its folded surface.

Steven sighed. "All right then, we'll go with the plan as it is. We'll call your parents and get instructions from them. Jack, we'll go snorkeling later. Got it?"

"Sure," Jack muttered. He sipped his orange juice, surprised at how bitter it tasted. Ashley didn't seem to mind the intrusion—in fact, she kept smiling at Forrest as if he were a rock star. For some reason, that got under Jack's skin worse than the change of plans.

After breakfast they walked to Park Headquarters, down uneven streets that wound lazily toward the sea as if they couldn't be troubled to get there in a straight line. Trees hung over cracked sidewalks, providing pools of shade that already felt good at nine in the morning. Old cars rattled by, kids ambled toward their elementary school, and young men moved along the street in packs, while middle-aged ladies walked past in dresses the color of jewels. The buildings in the city of Cruz Bay were small and painted in pastels, but tired looking, as if they'd stayed out too late at a party.

"Forrest, look at those flowers!" Ashley exclaimed, pointing to a bush exploding with orange and pink blossoms. "I've never seen anything like that before."

When Forrest didn't reply, Olivia answered for him. "Yes, they are lovely! They look as if they're growing wild. Imagine having blossoms like that come up in your yard without having to plant them. This really is an amazing place. Oh, I think I see Park Headquarters, right up ahead, by the dock."

A tall flagpole with an American flag identified the low-slung building. Small boats bobbed nearby, like white corks. In the distance, majestic cruise liners pushed through the water, big as castles. Sleek boats with tall masts and full sails glided past, propelled by the soft breeze. There seemed to be as many different kinds of boats as people on St. John—an entire world jumbled together on one island.

"You must be the Landon family," a black woman beamed as they entered the headquarters building. "Hello to you all. I'm Denise Georges. You're Forrest. Welcome," she said, shaking Forrest's hand firmly. "And you're Ashley?" she asked, as she moved down the line.

"Uh-huh."

"And Jack?"

"Hi," Jack said, shaking her hand.

When Denise turned her attention on Olivia, her forehead furrowed deep. "One thing confuses me in all of this, Dr. Landon. Your husband said you had a meeting this morning, but that was rescheduled for one o'clock two weeks ago. Didn't you get the message?"

Olivia's eyes widened. "I—no."

"Oh, man, we could have gone snorkeling after all," Jack moaned.

"Jack—enough with the snorkeling!" Steven said.

Denise turned her warm eyes on Jack. "So, you like to dive beneath the waves?"

"Like it? I love it. That's all I thought about coming over, but now…." He left his sentence dangling. Now Forrest had entered the picture, and everything was different, like a room that had tilted and everything in it was running downhill.

"Well then, if I might make a suggestion," Denise began. "Take my Jeep and go snorkeling this morning. Forrest can use my snorkel gear—it's in the back of the Jeep. While your dad's trying to get through to Paris, your mother can drive you to a wonderful snorkeling spot called Jumbie Bay. When you get back, I'll take you three kids on a tour while your mother is in her meeting. How does that sound?"

Olivia hesitated, but Jack could tell she looked pleased. "I don't know. Steven?"

"Fine with me. That's very generous of you, Denise."

Please, Mom? Jack asked her without saying a word. Smiling, Olivia finally nodded. Only Forrest, who stood off to the side, didn't smile.

#

Eighteen inches of Atlantic Ocean covered Jack's feet, but he could see his toes as clearly as if he were looking through glass. The gentle waves at Jumbie Bay were the most transparent he'd ever seen.

"Jumbie!" Ashley had exclaimed. "That's weird. I've

heard of Jumbo—like Jumbo the Clown or jumbo hot-dogs—but I've never heard of Jumbie."

Forrest frowned. "I think I've heard that word…," he began. "Once, maybe. A long time ago." Then, looking puzzled, he added, "I can't remember."

Ashley seemed pleased that Forrest was talking again. "Have you been snorkeling before?" she asked.

"Twice, once in California and once in the Bahamas. We're not going to stay here too long, are we?"

"Why are you in such a hurry?" Jack asked him. "Does it have something to do with the big secret and the danger and all of that?"

"What danger?" Ashley asked.

"Nothing." Dropping onto the sandy bottom, Jack struggled to pull on long, black swim fins, while the waves tried just as hard to wash them away. The fins were tight on his feet, but that was better than loose, because loose ones might slip off when he started swimming. Forrest had donned his fins back on the beach, which was not a very smart idea. Jack had to admit to feeling a certain satisfaction when he saw Forrest waddling awkwardly across the sand like a duck with big, webbed feet, flopping toward the water.

Except for the Landons and Forrest, Jumbie Bay was deserted. It had an ideal beach: Smooth, pale sand with enough trees along the edges for shade; a shallow, gradual descent into the clear water; schools of tiny fish visible less than ten feet from shore.

"Don't go too far out," Olivia warned them. "I want to be able to see all three of you at all times. Try to stay close together. And whatever you do, don't stand on the coral reefs. That will damage them. If you need to stand, make sure you're on the ocean bottom. If it's too deep there, just tread water."

They all nodded and moved farther out into the bay. Ashley'd been a great swimmer from as far back as Jack could remember, always gliding through water like a sleek, skinny seal. Now, resembling an aquatic astronaut with her mask over her eyes and nose and the snorkel tube in her mouth, she took the lead.

Deliberately, she kicked a splash of water at Jack, who was right behind her; he grabbed her ankle and gave it a hard tug. A minute later he noticed Forrest was swimming hard to get ahead of him. Let him! Why compete when the day was so perfect, the ocean so warm, the sun hot on his back, the fish so colorful?

Olivia swam up to them and bobbed in the water, taking the tube out of her mouth to say, "Have you seen all these fish? They're fantastic! Thousands of those little silversides, and the trumpetfish—I love trumpetfish. And those really bright ones are called parrotfish. But we should swim over toward the cliff, because that's where the reef is. Come on, follow me."

They did, paddling in a row after Olivia. Again the image of ducks flashed into Jack's mind: Olivia, the mamma duck, leading three baby ducks, but Jack and

Forrest were both bigger than Olivia. Only Ashley was still smaller than her mother.

Olivia had been right: When they came close to the cliff and peered down through the water, they saw coral, all kinds of coral. And lots more fish—one poking its face out from a little cave in the bottom of some brain coral; one with a gold stripe running from its eye to its tail like the racing stripes on a car; and three that had white stripes on black, like zebras. Others darting in front of Jack's face seemed close enough to touch but were always farther away than they looked.

Forrest grabbed Jack's arm, jerking him up out of the water. "Did you see them?" he yelled.

Ashley raised her head, too, and asked, "See what?"

"Squid. Two squid down there."

"You mean like giant octopuses with suckers on their tentacles that grab you and pull you down until you drown?" Ashley looked ready to swim back to shore.

"No, just squid. The kind they cut up for calamari in restaurants."

Jack didn't know what Forrest was talking about. Calamari? What was that? But he lowered his face mask to follow the direction where Forrest was pointing. He saw them, then, funny looking things like flying saucers with tails, only the tails were actually their arms and tentacles, all squeezed together. Eyes peered out from where the saucer part ended and the arms began. The squid shot through the water like little torpedoes.

The coral caught his attention next. He knew the name of at least one species—elkhorn coral. It looked just like the horns of the stag elks that wintered on the refuge where his mother worked. Brain coral was also easy to spot. It really did resemble a brain lifted out of someone's skull and dumped on the ocean floor. Other corals waved in the gentle current like fans.

When Jack raised his head out of the water to search for Ashley, he saw her far ahead, a good 50 feet away. She was waving wildly, beckoning them, mouthing the word "Hurry!" but not shouting it.

Jack and Forrest and Olivia swam toward her, wondering what she'd found. When they reached her, Ashley whispered, "There's a sea turtle swimming around down here. Not like the one we saw in Hawaii, Jack. This is a different kind. Different colors."

It was as if the turtle had been waiting for them to arrive to admire it. Moving leisurely through the clear water, it waved its long front legs effortlessly, while the Landons and Forrest glided behind. For what must have been ten minutes, they played follow-the-leader with the turtle. Then it disappeared into a haze of algae.

"Wasn't that fantastic?" Ashley sputtered, trying to get the words out before she removed her mouthpiece. Jack and Forrest agreed, but Olivia frowned.

"Didn't you like it, Mom?" Ashley asked.

"Of course. Seeing the turtle was wonderful, Ashley. Thanks for calling us. That one was a hawksbill, and as I've told you, they're becoming rare. But I'm really upset about the condition of the reef right beneath us. Didn't you notice? It's all broken up."

No, Jack hadn't noticed. He'd been too intent on following the turtle.

"That's from boat groundings—boats pulling up here where they're not supposed to," Olivia told them. "And then they cause even more damage when they lower their anchors. From the amount of destruction to the reef right here, I'd say a lot of anchors have been dropped, and I don't know why. This isn't a place where any boat owner would want to tie up."

Jack dove down for a closer look. It was just as his mother had said: The reef beneath him lay crumbled like smashed concrete, uneven and lifeless.

"What time is it, Jack?" his mother asked when he came up.

He looked at his waterproof wristwatch. "It's almost noon, straight up."

"We've got to go. Anyway, you kids have had enough sun for one day, especially you, Jack."

His mother was right. Jack was the fairest-skinned of them all, but his arms didn't look too red.

"Wow! You ought to see your back," Ashley exclaimed. "I can see every spot where you missed putting sunscreen. You're as splotchy as that pufferfish we saw."

Forrest laughed. Jack scowled.

CHAPTER FIVE

They returned to Park Headquarters in time for Olivia's one o'clock meeting—but just barely. It had been hard to leave Jumbie Bay and all the beautiful underwater creatures.

Denise waited for them at the visitor center, an open-air building with large windows that allowed the ocean breeze to drift through. She looked up from behind her desk and smiled. "Hello to all. Mr. Landon left to get more film for his camera. He'll be right back, and then he wants to go to the meeting with you, Dr. Landon. I'll take care of the children."

"Thank you so much—" Olivia began, but Denise waved her off. "You go to your meeting. Hurry, now."

When the door had shut behind Olivia, Forrest stepped up and rested his elbows on the countertop, saying, "Did Mr. Landon contact my parents?"

"He didn't say. I'm sure he'll tell you all about it when he gets back. Ready for your tour of St. John?" After pushing some papers into a neat stack, Denise stood up. "The first thing we're going to do is pay a visit to Miss Amelia."

"Miss Amelia? Who's that?" Ashley asked.

"A woman as old as the island. She weaves baskets and tells her stories for our classes. To meet Miss Amelia is to understand who we were and who we are."

Forrest's face seemed to juggle several emotions. "Does this she know all the people on St. John?"

"Oh, yes. Miss Amelia knows everybody."

"Then I want to go see her," Forrest decided, as though the whole thing were up to him. He waved his hand to usher Jack and Ashley through the door.

Outside, the Jeep the Park Service had loaned them was waiting; when Denise opened the door, Forrest got in the front seat beside her. Jack and Ashley climbed into the back, carefully handling seat belt buckles that had already become too hot to touch.

"Did you like your snorkeling, Ashley?" Denise asked, gazing at her in the rearview mirror.

"We loved it—it's like a whole other world down there! I didn't want to come out of the water."

"Yes, well, by the looks of your brother, it's a good thing you did." Then, to Jack, "You're lookin' mighty pink, mon. You must always be careful of the island sun. Have you ever been on St. John before?"

The three of them shook their heads.

"You'll find there's much to learn about our island. The first thing you should know is that 54 percent of St. John is National Park. That bay where you were swimming this morning—that's part of the park, and so are most of the other beaches and bays. Only 5,000 people live here, which leaves a lot of room for wilderness." As she pulled the Jeep onto the main street, Denise continued, "The American millionaire Laurence Rockefeller donated 5,000 acres for a National Park here on St. John, but it has grown over the years. Virgin Islands National Park now includes almost 13,000 acres."

"My parents donated a painting to a museum once," Forrest remarked. "My father is a diplomat in Paris."

Jack rolled his eyes and murmured, "Here we go again," as Ashley punched his arm and gave him a look.

"It's a great thing to share what you have been blessed with," Denise remarked. "Miss Amelia, she doesn't have that much by way of material possessions, but many would say she is the richest woman on the island because she shares so much with the rest of us. She lives way up on the mountain, where we're going now. She's almost 85, but she keeps us all running."

Denise chattered as she drove, telling them about the healing properties of native plants as well as a funny story about mongooses, which were brought to St. John to kill the rats. What people forgot, she told them, was that rats come out during the day and mongooses come out at night, so the two species never waged war. "So now we have both rats *and* mongooses," she said.

As Denise drove off the paved road onto a dirt one, the Jeep began winding higher and higher up the volcanic mountain. Rich, orange-red dirt lined the swatch of road, with plants of every shade of green cascading from the sides. Struggling as it bumped through ruts and around hairpin curves that twisted back onto themselves, the Jeep climbed higher and higher into the blue sky. It seemed impossible that an old woman like Miss Amelia could live in such a remote area.

"You should know that Miss Amelia still cuts cane with a knife and weaves baskets by hand," Denise told them. "She is a very strong woman. And she knows about the Jumbies."

"Jumbies?" Ashley asked. "You mean like Jumbie Bay where we were this morning? What are Jumbies?"

"Evil spirits. They are thick on the island. Miss Amelia can tell you all about them."

"I don't believe in spirits," Forrest stated. "Those stories are for the ignorant."

A smile curling the edges of her lips, Denise asked, "You're sure of that, are you? Well now, Miss Amelia might convince you differently. And here we are."

"Look at all the goats!" Ashley exclaimed. A dozen scrawny animals picked their way through old tires and bottles piled along the edge of a dilapidated fence. Uneven wooden stairs made their way up to the front door, but some were missing, like broken teeth on a comb. The house itself, a wooden rectangular box with peeling blue paint, looked run-down, but then, Miss Amelia was probably too old to fix up the place.

"The goats belong to Miss Amelia," Denise told them as she turned off the motor. "She doesn't have a phone, so I couldn't tell her I was bringing guests with me today. Wait here until I wave you in."

"May I pet the goats?" Ashley asked.

"Certainly. Just remember, they'll eat your clothes right off you, so keep a watchful eye. I'll be right back."

Jack and Ashley scrambled out, but Forrest moved more slowly, his eyes on the dirt road. "There's goat droppings all over the place," he complained.

"The droppings won't hurt you, Forrest," Ashley told him. "Come and pet the goats. They look friendly."

"No, thank you." Leaning against the Jeep, Forrest surveyed the land around him, his hand shielding his eyes from the bright sunlight.

"Come on," Ashley urged. "I bet you've never met a goat."

"True. But I don't particularly want to meet a goat."

"I'll go," Jack told his sister, annoyed that she hadn't asked him in the first place. He followed her 50 feet up the hill to the knot of goats. One of the animals nibbled Jack's shorts before he pushed its head away. Ashley clucked at the animal, then turned to Jack, keeping her voice low as she asked, "I've been wanting to talk to you alone ever since breakfast. What's going on? Why don't you like Forrest?"

"Who says I don't?"

"Come on, it's obvious. You looked like you wanted to burn him into toast at breakfast. What's up with that?"

"I don't know. Last night he started talking, and he said some stuff that was just…weird," Jack began, rubbing the patch of hair between a goat's nubby horns.

"Like what?"

"Like how he knows some big secret he can't tell because it would be dangerous for me to be in on it."

"Are you serious?"

Shrugging, Jack said, "I kept asking him to tell me what he meant, but he wouldn't. It sounds really crazy."

"Are you going to tell Mom and Dad?"

Jack considered this. "No. I said I wouldn't. I don't believe him, anyway—he's just talking to make himself sound like he's 'all that.'"

"I know he's different," Ashley said. "But he's kind of amazing, too. Just give him a chance, OK? He's not any worse than a lot of our other foster kids."

"I know. I just hope he'll be gone soon."

"Jack!"

"What?" Jack flared. "Can't I tell you what I think of Forrest without you getting all—"

"That's not what I meant. Look! There's Miss Amelia." She pointed to the top of the rickety stairs where a large woman stood next to Denise. Gray-white hair curled from the edge of a scarf that covered most of her head, while a yellow cotton dress billowed around her legs. Miss Amelia opened wide her arms and in a deep, rich, Caribbean lilt, called to them, "Boys and one little girl, I call you welcome to Miss Amelia's house. Come!"

"Let's go!" Ashley took off in the lead, with Jack trailing her and Forrest lagging behind. When they'd climbed the wooden stairs, Denise ushered them to a side deck. Baskets filled with dyed reeds crowded like giant toadstools around a wooden glider, while slivers of freshly cut cane curled across the floor. Several buckets held water and sliced cane. Half-formed baskets, one with a red-and-green pattern and two of combined yellow, green, and orange, had been set on the floor, their ribs reaching into the air like bony fingers. Everything was a colorful, jumbled-up mess.

Forrest picked his way uneasily to the chair farthest from the glider, brushing off the surface before sitting down. "There's a lizard—right there, on the wall!" he cried, jumping to his feet and pointing.

"So there is," Miss Amelia answered. "That lizard, he tell you to sit closer."

Though he looked unhappy about it, Forrest pulled his chair next to the glider. Jack, Ashley, and Denise found three stools and crowded close as Miss Amelia settled herself, picking up a long piece of reed and turning it. The dark skin of her hands was filled with tiny scars patterned like stars.

"Miss Amelia," Denise said loudly, "These are the children I told you about."

"Yes, yes," Miss Amelia answered, gesturing with the small knife in her right hand. "They nice children."

"I told them how you make the baskets," Denise said. "Will you show us? And maybe share with us some of your stories. Tell us about when you were young. The island was very different then."

"Could you tell us about the Jumbies?" Ashley pleaded. "I want to hear Jumbie stories."

"Ah, you know Jumbies?" Miss Amelia's brown face broke into a smile. Pulling a piece of vine from a basket, she placed her knife at the end and deftly sliced it in half. Although her knuckles were large and misshapen, she had nimble fingers. Jack was impressed at the perfect cut she made.

"First I tell you about the baskets," she said. "I use the hoop vine to make them. You cannot cut it until the dark side of the moon, at low tide. The red dye, it come from a cactus plant. The yellow is poisonous—that's from the bark of a tree. The green is not a dye only—it is a medicine also, good for rash on your skin, sunburn, and mosquito bite."

"You could use some of that stuff on your sunburn," Denise commented to Jack. Then, to Miss Amelia, "Tell them how many were in your family."

"Fifteen children—we lived in a small house with no electricity, no running water." She took the vine and sliced the half in half again, the blade flashing in the sun. "For shopping, we had to go from here down the mountain. I used to get up at five o'clock in the morning and go to Coral Bay—only one shop was there. The shopkeeper give me everything that my mother have on the list. First I put the towel on my head, and then I take the basket with all the things in it and put it on my head. I walk the path alone to my home, one foot in front of the other. If a bird fly it, it would be five mile. But I am no bird."

"How old were you?" Jack asked.

"Seven."

"Child abuse," Forrest muttered, shaking his head.

Miss Amelia smiled serenely and said, "I look back today, and I thank my mother for bringing me up the way she did—hard. She say, 'Child, you don't know what the future is ahead. If you find hardship, you already passed through it, so it will be no bother to you.' And I be glad of that. I didn't fear the work, but now…." With her worn hands, she patted her knees. "These won't allow me to get around the way I want to. Sometimes they not too good."

She looked off in the distance, as though remembering when her knees were young and strong. "In my days growing up, it was living happy, because I wasn't afraid of nothing. You think my life was bad, Forrest? Not true. We was more happy then than today. We wasn't afraid of nothing but the Jumbies."

Forrest replied, "I already explained to Denise that I don't believe in Jumbies."

Miss Amelia made another perfect slice of the hoop vine. "You do not have to believe. But the Jumbies, they believe in you."

Looking skeptical, Forrest slid down in his seat. Why couldn't he just listen to the stories like the rest of them, Jack wondered. Miss Amelia wove her words into patterns as beautiful as her baskets, and whether or not her stories were true, it was kind of her to share.

"More stories, please," Ashley begged. Everywhere the Landons went, Ashley tried to find tales told by park interpretive rangers or by people who lived in the area.

"I tell you about one time when I was a child, and I walk home from Cruz Bay," Miss Amelia said. "The sun was playing on the sea—it was late. I know that night was going to catch me on the road, so I run much of the way. Then, coming in over where that big locust tree is—" Miss Amelia pointed. "A spirit was there."

All of them turned to stare at the locust tree.

"Now I hear my mother always speak about that spirit. And when I get to the tree, I look up, and I see a face. I look for the foot—no foot, only the head. I hear footsteps coming behind me, but when I look behind me, there was nothing there. And I couldn't move. I freeze with fright. Then somebody come behind me and push me."

As Miss Amelia's hands, which had been busy

slicing, suddenly stopped in midair, Jack felt cold fingers prick at his skin. Ashley, too, looked at Miss Amelia with wide eyes.

"A spirit pushed you," Denise broke in.

"Yes. I say, 'Leave me be,' but the spirit, it get closer, and I yell, *'Mamma!'* And she be far away, but she say, 'I comin'.' She know that I was in trouble. By the time I get to her, she say to me, 'What you doin' with all these people behind you?'"

Ashley gasped.

"And when the morning come I say, 'Mamma, who those people were?' And she say, 'They were the dead. It was your grandmother who shoved you. She saved you from the Jumbies.' That is a true story."

Nodding, Miss Amelia picked up another vine, this time bending it around her knee to form it into the shape of a rainbow. "Yes, on my island, the dead talk with the living. My mother told me of a spirit who came to her one night. The spirit told her, 'A dark one will be born on our island. She will be of the past and the present, the future and the past, black with white. The stars, they will guide her, and she will make people free.' And it came true. And the two of us—the dark one and me—we make the people free."

"What you talkin', Miss Amelia?" Denise asked. "Who do you make free? I don't know that part of your story."

"You think I tell you everything, child? Oh, there is much about me you do not know. I love you like my own, Denise, but I never tell you everything. No." Using the end of the vine like a skeletal finger, she suddenly pointed at Forrest and said, "There is seeing, and there is seeing. What is it you see, child?" Her large, owl-like eyes gazed at him. The air seemed to swell with the heat as they all waited for Forrest to reply.

"I...I don't understand her question," Forrest said to Denise. "What does she want?"

"She's asking what you believe in—what guides you."

"I guess I believe that if something's going to happen, it's up to me to make it happen," he answered slowly. "I believe in me. I make my own magic."

Miss Amelia picked up a half-finished basket, its ribs sticking up naked and alone. With amazing speed, she began to weave a piece of vine in and out of the ribs, pulling hard as she twisted the piece around a corner. In, out, in, out, tug—Jack could hardly keep up, watching the swiftness of her fingers as Miss Amelia wove another row.

"Uh, uh, uh," she said. "Why don't you ask me, son?"

"Are you talking to me?" Forrest pointed a finger at his own chest.

"Yes. Now you ask me the question that has been troubling you. What is it you want?"

Forrest's lips trembled. Confused, he looked from Jack to Ashley, then to Miss Amelia. "I—I need to find someone. How did you—Miss Amelia, do you know a woman by the name of...Cimmaron?"

Miss Amelia smiled at him. "Yes. I know this woman. She tell the stories she hear from her grandmother's grandmother's grandmother's grandmother, from long ago when our people were slaves. I teach this woman how to make baskets, and she tell me things. She works in the Paradise Motel. She be waiting for you." A hummingbird buzzed by, coming within inches of Forrest's head before darting off again. Miss Amelia smiled. "The hummingbird bring you luck, bring you to our island. My friend the storyteller, Cimmaron, she tell me so."

Miss Amelia's fingers never stopped moving over the basket. She seemed unaware that her words had caused Forrest to become as rigid as a statue.

"What is it?" Ashley asked Forrest. "What's wrong? Who's Cimmaron?"

Forrest's lips moved, but his next words were almost inaudible.

"What did you say?" Ashley pressed.

"She's—she's my mother. Cimmaron is my mother."

CHAPTER SIX

The upholstery in the Jeep was hot. As they bumped along another winding dirt road, Jack felt as if he were sitting on a griddle. Still, he didn't feel he could ask Denise to turn up the air-conditioning: That would interrupt the conversation between Forrest and Ashley. Ashley had begun to pry out of Forrest the details of the mystery he'd refused to talk about the night before.

"So, you're saying your *birth* mother is from St. John?"

"Yes. I was born here, 13 years ago. On January 21st. This is my island."

"It sounds like you've always known about her—your birth mother, I mean. That part wasn't a secret, right?"

Forrest nodded. He looked out the window for a moment before answering. "I've always known that her name was Cimmaron. Except for her name, I don't know anything about her. I was told that when I was less than a year old, Forrest Winthrop III and his wife, Hilary Danforth Winthrop, adopted me from this island. The Winthrops told me about my place of origin, but they always said they didn't want me to ever come back here because that was my past and they are my future. But now…." He slammed his fist against the seat. "I *have* to talk to her! To Cimmaron!"

Nodding, Ashley asked, "Does she know about you? I mean, about you coming here to St. John? Miss Amelia kind of hinted that she might be expecting you."

Forrest shook his head. "That was just Miss Amelia's Jumbie superstition."

Ashley's hand fluttered to Forrest's shoulder. "Wow. So she doesn't even know you're here. Oh my gosh."

"But I can find her now that I know where she is. Denise, will you take me?"

Jack watched Denise stiffen. "That is not my place to do. No, no, no." She shook her head emphatically.

"Denise, please!"

"No!" Denise's arguments sounded solid: They might not even have the right Cimmaron, and if they did, the Landons should be the ones to take him; she was only a park ranger and couldn't interfere; his adoptive parents needed to be informed before Forrest contacted Cimmaron; and Cimmaron might not want to meet with Forrest at all, so at the very least she was due a phone call, not a surprise visit. Every argument was met with an equally persuasive one from Forrest: The Landons were not his legal guardians, which meant he was still technically on his own; he'd flown almost 3,000 miles to St. John by himself, so why stop him when he was only 5 miles away from his birth mother; if he waited too long, Cimmaron might be gone, and he absolutely had to talk to her for a reason he couldn't share but that was extremely important. Jack's mind snapped back to—was it only this morning?—when Forrest had told him he knew something dangerous.

But how could Forrest know something dangerous about Cimmaron? He hadn't even known how to find her until Miss Amelia told him where she worked. Jack pushed down his uneasy feeling and listened to Forrest's final argument: If he gave Cimmaron a heads-up, she might refuse to meet with him, and he couldn't take the chance that she would disappear from him forever.

No matter what Forrest tried, Denise wouldn't budge. "It's not up to me," she told him again and again. "Let the day play out, and the Landons will take you where you need to go."

"So it doesn't matter what I want," Forrest said wearily. "She's that close, and you won't help me." He leaned his forehead into the window of the car, and Jack could see the utter frustration etched on his face.

Trying to quiet Forrest, Denise said, "I'll tell you what I *will* do. This is your island, and we are your people. Let me tell you about our history, Forrest. I'll take you all to a place with a strange past, a place where the slaves made the rum. It's beautiful to see, but its story is dark. The rum was made with the blood of slaves."

"Really?" Ashley breathed. "Forrest, that sounds amazing. Don't you think that sounds amazing?"

Forrest didn't move.

"Metaphorically speaking, the rum was made from blood," Denise added, and smiled.

As they drove, Jack watched wild tangles of undergrowth grow thinner as the hillside melted away. Suddenly he saw bright blue water far below. The waves curled onto the white sands of the shore. It was as startling as a painting, as if a corner of heaven had fallen to Earth. The view might have calmed Forrest, but he didn't see it because he'd squeezed his eyes shut.

"Children, we are here," Denise told them as she parked under a leafy tree. "We're going to walk to this overlook so you can see some other islands. You're looking north now, at the British Virgin Islands. That's the island of Tortola in the distance," she said, pointing, "and the water you're seeing is the Atlantic Ocean."

"It is? I thought it was the Caribbean Sea," Ashley said. "Forrest, didn't you think it was the Caribbean Sea?"

No answer.

Denise cleared her throat. "On the south side it's the Caribbean, but on the north is the Atlantic."

To check it out, Jack studied a map of St. John he'd picked up earlier at the visitor center. There it was— the Atlantic. He liked finding Tortola on the map, then glancing up to see the actual island across the water.

"Uh-oh," he said, "there's a misprint on the map."

"Where?" Denise asked. "That's a National Park map. It better be correct."

"Right here," Jack answered, pointing at the small print. "This place that's right to the east of us—it says Water*lemon* Cay instead of Watermelon Cay. Somebody got a few letters mixed up."

Denise grabbed his shoulder playfully and shook it. "You scared me for a minute. That's no mistake. It's *supposed* to be Waterlemon Cay. That's its name. Waterlemon is the fruit of a tropical plant called *Passiflora laurifolia.* It has purple flowers and yellow berries that you can eat."

That Denise—she knew everything. Jack felt kind of dumb for declaring that the map was wrong. He thought he saw a smile play at the edges of Forrest's mouth, but it was gone before Jack could be sure. Well, at least his mistake had gotten Forrest to smile and that was an improvement over his sullen silence.

"Now we're going to the Annaberg Sugar Plantation," Denise announced. "It's all part of the park. We have to walk a little way, so I'll tell you about it as we go."

"Another story?" Ashley asked, hopeful.

"A bit of history," Denise answered. "This place where we are right now was once a plantation that grew sugarcane to make molasses—and rum. Two hundred years ago, traders used rum like we use cash today.

You could buy anything with it—including people."

"People?"

"Yes, Ashley. Slaves."

That caught Forrest's attention. Ahead of them stood a tall, cone-shaped structure. "That used to be a windmill," Denise told them. "It once had sails that turned around to make power that pressed the juice from sugarcane to make sugar, and, like I said, molasses and rum."

"And the slaves had to do all the hard labor, right?" Forrest asked, finally breaking his silence. "What were their lives like? Horrible?"

"Not always. When this plantation was really producing, the slaves weren't so bad off. Anyway, who do you think built all this?" She gestured around her at the roofless buildings, the kitchen house, the crumbling factory walls. "It wasn't the Europeans who built it, you can be sure. It was the Africans. They were strong and smart."

Walking toward the windmill, she pointed to the curved walls and said, "Tell me what you think is holding these bricks together."

"Mortar," Jack answered. "Cement."

"It's mortar, all right, but not the kind of cement you know about. To make this stuff, the black people went to the ocean and removed hard coral. They burned it and mixed it with shells, stone, goat hair—and molasses. We have the sweetest ruins in the world. But don't try to eat them." She laughed at her own joke.

"A hundred and sixty years ago," she went on,

"when this plantation was flourishing, the slaves could grow their own crops and sell them to get money to buy their freedom. Some were already free. A lot of people have a lot of foolish thoughts that everybody black was a slave, but that isn't true."

Forrest stared at her intently, as she continued.

"In 1848, all the slaves on St. John were set free, almost 20 years before slavery ended in the United States. They were poor, but most were happy. Very different from what it was like way before that, back in 1733." Denise frowned, and her voice rose as she told them, "Back in those bad old days of the 1700s, when the island was called St. Jan, it was torture to be a slave. That's why they revolted."

"Revolted?" That from Ashley, again sensing a story.

"Yes. Some slaves had been proud, noble warriors in Africa and would not bow down before any man."

Jack couldn't help think how strange it was that something as trivial as the shade of a person's skin could determine someone's whole life. "What happened when they wouldn't bow down?" he asked.

"Look over there." Denise directed their attention to a spit of land jutting out to the north. "Many of the ones who couldn't bear to be slaves killed themselves by jumping off the cliff right there onto the rocks on the shore. Others leaped from a place called Rams Head."

Clenching his fists, Forrest said softly, "They chose death over slavery."

"Yes, but any time you read about African history, remember, Africans did not write their own stories. They were written by Europeans, and sometimes the writers didn't know the truth. Go to the source, I always say. And that leads us back to Cimmaron. She's a story-teller, you know. I think you need to proceed with this quest of yours, Forrest, but you need to do it the right way. I'm taking you all back to the Landons."

Jack was surprised that Forrest didn't object. As the four of them walked toward the Jeep, Forrest was not only quiet, he also seemed rather pleased with himself.

The closer they got to the Jeep, the more Denise fumbled in agitation through the pockets of her green, park ranger shorts. "What did I do with those keys?" she muttered. "Are the Jumbies bothering me today?

While the kids stood waiting beside the Jeep, Denise became more and more perplexed. "I lost the stupid keys!" she cried. "We have to go back the way we came and look on the ground. Come on, you kids, help me search. Your eyes are young and sharp."

They spread out a little, walking slowly toward the windmill, around the ruins of the other buildings, and finally to the observation point where Denise had shown them the British Virgin Islands to the north.

Jack had been focusing on the ground, but when he looked up, he saw Forrest standing on the stone and mortar wall that bordered the overlook, poised like an orator ready to make a speech.

"Wa ju do up dere?" Denise demanded, falling into the native speech.

Forrest stood with his right side facing them. Slowly, he raised his left arm in the direction of the Atlantic. From his fingers dangled the Jeep keys.

"You want these back?" he asked. "Then take me to Cimmaron. Now!"

"Why, you little toad," Denise spat. "Give me those keys."

"Forrest, don't," Ashley cried, fear gripping her face. "My mom and dad will help you find Cimmaron, I know they will. You're not going to jump, are you?"

Forrest just laughed at her. "No, Ashley, I'm not going to jump. I'm not that desperate. But remember how I told you I was a star athlete at school? You should see how far I can throw these keys. Practically all the way to Tortola—if Denise refuses to negotiate. After all, I know all about negotiating. My father is a diplomat."

There was no one else around, no tourist they could ask for a ride. It was spring break, and the island was full of college kids partying in Cruz Bay or sleeping till afternoon to be ready to party again that night. Denise had a cell phone she could use to call for help, but it was locked inside the Jeep. Forrest really had them.

"Come on, Forrest, give Denise the keys," Jack urged.

"I'm not negotiating with you, Jack. This is between me and Denise."

"Oh it is, is it?" Denise stood with her hands on her

hips, like a statue carved from fine mahogany, staring at Forrest. She was one impressive woman, with her close-cropped hair, as short as Forrest's, her dangling earrings that weren't likely to be part of a regulation Park Service uniform, and a silver ring on the thumb of her right hand. She looked like she wouldn't take nonsense from anyone. And yet....

"If I agreed to do what you want and take you to Cimmaron," she said to Forrest, "how do you know I wouldn't be lying? I could get the keys and drive you straight back to Park Headquarters."

Staring back at her, Forrest answered, "Because you and I—we're alike. We are people of honor."

A small smile played around Denise's lips.

"I need this, Denise. It's more important than you could ever guess. Just give me five minutes with my mother. I promise I won't cause you any more trouble. I'll do what you want, go where you want. But I'm asking you...." Making a fist around the keys, he slowly extended his hand toward Denise. "Do this for me. Do this for her. Please."

Time seemed to crawl as Denise weighed what to do. Forrest's gaze never wavered, and Jack wondered how he could keep such perfect balance, as if he had rooted himself into the molasses mortar.

Finally, Denise shook her head. "Come on, mon," she said. "Jump down here quick and give me the keys. We'll go find your Cimmaron."

CHAPTER SEVEN

The Paradise Motel was an old, three-story building on a corner lot downtown. Weeping trees surrounded the Paradise like weary sentinels, their thick, ancient trunks blocking most of the view from the street. As with many of the buildings in St. John, the stucco had been painted Pepto-Bismol pink. A sign dangling from a wrought-iron pole showed where to check in with a painted hand pointing to a set of glass double doors.

"Well," Forrest said, peering out of the Jeep. "Here it is. The Paradise." He looked scared to death.

"Yes, here it is," Denise agreed. She pulled into an alley across the way. As she slid the gear into "park," she turned to ask Forrest, "You sure you want to do this now? Because there's still time to leave."

Although Forrest looked anything but sure, he nodded. "Yes, I'm ready."

"All right then. Come on, let's see what's waiting for us. It could be nothing, it could be everything, but we'll never know sitting here in the Jeep," Denise told them.

As they climbed out of the backseat, Jack let Forrest take the lead. This was Forrest's story, not his, and in a way he felt he shouldn't be there at all. Denise, too, kept a step behind. Jack noticed once again how strong she looked. Her calf muscles rippled as she walked. Forrest, who was already as tall as Denise, appeared spindly in comparison. His feet, encased in expensive sneakers, seemed too big for the rest of him, like a puppy who hadn't yet grown into its paws.

"I hope Cimmaron will be OK with this," Ashley whispered.

"Me, too," Jack answered.

"You know, not all birth mothers want to be found. What if she won't talk to him?"

"I'm more worried that we've got the wrong Cimmaron. I think that would be really hard on Forrest."

Ashley pursed her lips as she waited for a car to chug by. Forrest and Denise were already across the street, walking slowly up the path to the entrance to the Paradise. Checking right, then left, because in St. John the cars ran the opposite way from they way they do on the U.S. mainland, Ashley stepped into the street. "Since when do you care about Forrest?" she asked Jack.

The question surprised him, because it was true things had changed, and he didn't know when or where.

No, that wasn't true, he did know. It began back at Miss Amelia's, when Forrest heard Cimmaron's name and told them she was his mother. It was at the sugar plantation, when he'd boldly struck a bargain with Denise. For all of his attitude problems, Forrest had guts. Watching him, seeds of respect had been planted in Jack, who truly wanted this reunion to go well.

"I guess he's not so bad," Jack mumbled.

"It's weird, thinking of what's about to happen. Unless she's already left for the day, Cimmaron is inside that building, only moments away from meeting her son."

"*If* we have the right Cimmaron."

"Right. If."

Suddenly, thoughts of what could go wrong made Jack's stomach clamp. How must Forrest be feeling? As if in reply, Forrest stopped at the front door and waited for Jack and Ashley to catch up. His eyes were wide. Denise stood beside him, her face tranquil, like someone with all the time in the world.

"You want us to wait out here?" Jack asked.

"No. I'm afraid I'm going to back down. I need you to make me do this."

"No one can make you but yourself," Denise told him. "This is your call."

"Right." Forrest took a deep breath and put his hand on the brass doorknob. "Let's do it."

The lobby inside the Paradise was small, filled with European-style furniture that seemed strangely out of place in the tropics. Two ornate chairs, both covered in maroon velvet, sat opposite a couch embroidered with a scene from a fox hunt. A large, carved desk stood at one end with a sign that read Registration.

"May I help you?" a young man asked pleasantly. The badge he wore said Toby.

"Uh, yes." Forrest cleared his throat. "Is there a maid here, I mean, a woman by the name of—Cimmaron?"

"She's almost off duty. I just saw her ten minutes ago, so I believe she's still here." Toby looked expectantly from face to face. "Do you want me to call her?"

Forrest barely nodded. The young man punched a button on a phone, speaking into it, "This is the front desk. I have some visitors here for Cimmaron." There was a pause, and then Toby looked up. "Who shall I say is calling?"

When Forrest just stood there, blank, Jack stepped forward and told Toby, "Friends of Miss Amelia. We were just at her house. She told us to come."

"Friends of Miss Amelia," Toby repeated. "All right, I'll tell them." He hung up the phone. "She'll be right down. Please, make yourselves comfortable in the lobby. It will only be a moment."

"Thank you," Forrest answered woodenly.

Jack sat on the sofa, feeling as stiff as the tapestry that rubbed against his skin. Forrest, his hands clenched behind his back, wandered from painting to painting, pretending to be interested in the reproductions. Denise and Ashley sat in the chairs, facing Jack. No one spoke. Moments later, a door swung open, and a black woman entered. She was tall and thin, with thick hair pulled back into a bushy ponytail.

She was beautiful. High cheekbones set off large, almond eyes that looked coolly from one face to the next. While Forrest's skin was the color of creamed coffee, Cimmaron's was a dark mocha. Head high, back straight in perfect posture, it seemed as though she were the owner of the Paradise rather than the one who cleaned the rooms. Walking directly to Denise, she said, "Miss Amelia, she sent you?"

"Not me," Denise replied, pointing to Forrest. "Him."

Cimmaron turned. If Jack had expected instant recognition, mother to son, he was wrong. Cimmaron, her weight on one leg and her elbow resting on her jutting hip, looked at Forrest. "Well?" she demanded.

"My name is…uh…Forrest." He said it so quietly that Cimmaron might not have heard. A little louder, he added, "I live in Denver, in the United States."

"If it's baskets you be wanting, Miss Amelia's are better. Mine are strictly amateur."

Forrest flinched. "No, I didn't come for baskets. Um—is there somewhere we could go? To talk? What I want to say is—private."

"Whatever you want to tell me, you can do it here." Cimmaron looked at Forrest through narrowed eyes.

Toby, who'd been watching from the desk, cleared

his throat. "Nobody's around right now, so I think I'll go back and grab a cup of coffee. Will one of you come get me if a guest arrives?"

"I will," Ashley volunteered, raising her hand.

"Good. I'll be right through those doors there." With that, Toby disappeared, leaving the five of them alone in the lobby.

After hesitating, Forrest took a step toward Cimmaron. It could have been Jack's imagination, but he thought he saw a clear resemblance between the two. Cimmaron had the same perfect bone structure, the same lean build, the same way of holding her head so that every inch of her height counted. But it was more than just the physical—there was a fire inside them, a nobility, that mirrored flame to flame.

"Who are the others?" Jack knew she meant him and Ashley and Denise.

Without hesitation, Forrest answered, "My friends."

"You want them here?" Cimmaron's face betrayed no emotion.

"I do. Maybe we should...could we sit down?"

Jack jumped off the couch to offer it to them, but Cimmaron waved him off. "There is no need. I will stand. Why don't you just come out with it and ask me whatever it is you're going to ask me? What has happened—has the cat got your tongue?"

It looked as though Forrest didn't know what to say. For once, words seemed to dry up inside him. Eyes wide, fists jammed against his sides, he stood silent.

Cimmaron's chin tipped toward the ceiling. "Since you're afraid to speak, let me see if I can guess. You're here looking for your birth mother. Am I right?"

His mouth barely moving, Forrest croaked, "Yes."

"You want to ask me about January 21st, the day you were born. You come all the way from the United States to ask me this. To find your roots. To find your blood." A beat later, she added, "To find me."

Forrest's voice sounded strangely flat. "So I was right. You are my—mother." His shoulders sagged, as if he'd gone soft in the middle.

"I am the one who bore you. Your mother is some-one else. Why did you do this to me?" Cimmaron looked almost angry, and Jack's mind flashed to what his sis-ter had said only moments before. Some people didn't want to be found. It looked as if Cimmaron was one of those. "You are not mine, not any longer," she went on defiantly. "Why stir up the past?"

Forrest squeezed his eyes shut, and Jack wondered if it was to hold back tears. He felt suddenly angry. Why did Cimmaron have to be so cold? There was no need for Forrest to have to stand there as if he were naked in front of them all; there was no purpose in making him squirm. What mother wouldn't want to meet her own child?

"Maybe we should go," Jack said out loud. When it seemed as though no one heard, he stayed in his seat.

One way or another, the scene would have to play out.

"You do this to bring me pain," Cimmaron said, again defiant. "I have enough pain. You do not need to bring more."

"No, not for...I needed to...there are many reasons. Why did you give me up?" he asked abruptly.

Now it was Cimmaron who seemed to flag. "I gave you away so you could have a better life. Your parents, they have been good to you?"

Forrest didn't answer.

"They promised me," she said, her voice tight. "They said they could give you a better life."

"I have money. I'm educated. But it doesn't change the fact that you—you didn't want me."

"Child, child, of course I wanted you. But life is hard. We all do what we must do."

"Is that 'must' or 'want'?"

Before she could answer, the door to the lobby opened. An elderly couple came inside, pulling two suitcases as if they were dogs on a leash. The man, dressed in a bright orange shirt, looked around expectantly. The woman fussed behind him about how much he'd tipped the cabbie, until she realized the front desk was empty. "Now look, there's no one here to give us a room. How are we going to check in?"

In a flash, Ashley was on her feet. "Toby just stepped out for a minute. I'll get him for you."

"Oh, thank you, dear," the woman clucked.

While Ashley vanished behind the door, Denise went to where Forrest stood and placed a hand gently on his shoulder. "Perhaps it would be better if we moved to another place," she said quietly. Then, to Cimmaron, "Are you hungry? There's a restaurant where we could go eat, on the street right across from the Park Service. The Songbird. Do you know it?"

"Of course," Cimmaron said, nodding tersely.

"Then I suggest we continue the conversation there. When you get settled I can run and get the Landons—"

"Who are they?" Cimmaron demanded.

"It's a long story. Forrest can explain. It would be better if we go now. All right?"

Forrest seemed to hold his breath until Cimmaron finally agreed, saying, "But I want to take my own car. I'll meet you there." With that, Cimmaron turned and walked through the door. She never looked back.

#

The Songbird restaurant had an outside terrace filled with tables that had large green umbrellas. Two sets of stone steps led to the patio, where customers could sit and watch the harbor ships while sipping a cool drink. It was nice, and, Jack realized as he glanced at the menu, expensive. "I'm buying," Forrest announced, as if he could read Jack's mind. "Order whatever you want."

"Oh, no, the bill will be too high, " Denise protested as she sank into her chair. "I thought we could just buy a Coke and wait for Cimmaron."

"Don't worry about cost. I've got plenty of money."

For some reason, Forrest's remark didn't set Jack's teeth on edge this time. It was just a fact, like saying he had brown eyes. Since Jack was starving, he quickly decided to accept the offer, and he could tell by the way Ashley was studying the menu that she wanted to accept, too. As she glanced at him, Jack gave a quick nod. Ashley wiggled her eyebrows and went back to checking out the food items, smiling happily when she saw the picture of a giant, chocolate malt. When it came to food, Ashley could out-eat almost anyone.

Forrest had seated himself so that he could watch the street, which he did intently. Two open-air taxis puttered by, followed by a tour bus and a silver Mercedes. Throngs of people floated across the terrace below, the way petals floated in the breeze, some laughing, others linked arm in arm. Directly across the street, a wide concrete lot led to the Park Service building. Denise would be able to walk there in two minutes.

The waitress came by once, twice, then a third time to take their orders. Each time Forrest told her no, they were waiting for a fifth member of their party. After the fourth query, he reluctantly ordered. He barely touched his food when it was set in front of him.

By the time the plates were cleared, Forrest no longer watched the street. Instead, he took his straw and stabbed the cherry resting at the bottom of his glass until nothing remained but pulverized fragments. The few times Ashley tried to draw him out were met with stony silence. When Ashley asked if she could order a piece of key lime pie, Forrest only nodded. He seemed fascinated with his glass, running his finger across its rim as if daring it to sing. "She's not coming, is she," he finally said.

"It must have been a shock for her," Denise told him gently. "Don't take it too hard."

"She didn't want me then, and she doesn't want me now. It's obvious."

"No, that's not it. Cimmaron's got a lot to think about. Give her some space, Forrest." Glancing at her watch, Denise announced, "It is time now for us to find the Landons. The meeting should be over. Can you take your pie with you, Ashley?"

"Do I have to? I want to eat it sitting here, watching the boats."

"You go on, Denise," Jack told her. "I'll stay with Ashley."

"I prefer to remain as well," Forrest announced.

When Denise hesitated, Jack said, "We can get ourselves across the street. Go on. We'll be along soon."

"All right, then. No place else, understand? Finish the pie and then come straight over." Pushing back from the table, Denise stood quickly, which caused her earrings to swing furiously. "I have a lot of explaining to do to your parents. It might be better if I do it alone."

Moving easily, Denise half jumped down the stairs

and made her way across the street. Several people greeted her as she walked, and she answered each with a friendly wave. Soon she vanished into the Park Headquarters building.

"I hope Mom and Dad won't get mad that we went to see Cimmaron without them," Ashley began, taking a bite of the pale green pie filling. When she saw Forrest's expression, she quickly added, "But I know it'll be fine. They'll probably help you find her again—if you want that. Do you still want to see Cimmaron?"

Forrest shrugged. His eyes were fixed on his glass again, and this time he dropped bits of napkin into the cherry remains. What a messy thing to do, Jack thought. He was just thinking he should leave the waitress an extra tip when he heard an old blue Chevrolet rattle loudly up the street. He watched as it squeezed into a space that was too small for its size, rocking forward, then back, until it stopped with only inches to spare. The driver of the car got out and slammed the door, slinging a macramé purse over her shoulder. Her hair was unbound and wild, and her jewel-green sarong seemed alive in the ocean breeze.

Cimmaron had come.

CHAPTER EIGHT

"So you waited for me. You have tenacity." Dropping into Denise's empty chair, Cimmaron raised her hand to signal the waitress, who trotted over immediately. "Iced tea, please, with a twist of lemon."

"Certainly." Flipping out her order book, the waitress scribbled quickly, asking, "Would you like a menu?"

"No, thank you. I will not be staying."

Forrest's eyes—the same almond-shaped eyes as Cimmaron had—bored into her, but Cimmaron didn't return his gaze. She looked different out of uniform. Freed from the ponytail, her hair was much longer than Jack would have guessed, halfway down her back and tight with curls. A wooden necklace of sea creatures hung just past her collarbone, set off by earrings in the shape of starfish and a bracelet stamped with sand dollars. Cranberry lipstick had been painted carefully on her full lips, and there was a faint blush of color on her high cheekbones, yet she wore no eye makeup. An exotic mixture of gardenia and spice made her smell heavenly. The only thing that betrayed a life of hard work was her hands. The skin was dry and cracked, and her knuckles looked too large for her fingers.

It was Ashley who flared up. Rocking forward, her elbows on the table, she looked sternly at Cimmaron. "What do you mean, you're not staying? Why not? And why did you make Forrest sit here, wondering the whole time if you were coming? You should have seen him, staring at every car that went by. It was awful!"

"Ashley—" Jack began, sending his sister a warning look. He knew how her heart went out to anything hurt or injured. From abandoned wild creatures to kids at school who'd been bullied, she was always standing up for them and taking their part. But this was different. This was an adult she was ripping into.

Ignoring him, Ashley pushed on. "You know what? We almost left before you got here. What if we had gone? You don't even know where to find Forrest! He would have flown back to Denver thinking you didn't even care!"

"I don't answer to you, girl," Cimmaron said coolly. "I answer to no one but myself."

Forrest shot Ashley a grateful look that at the same time was a warning. "It's all right, Ashley. Really."

The waitress suddenly appeared, setting down the

glass of iced tea and chirping, "Is there anything else I can get you?" to which Cimmaron smiled and replied, "No. Thank you."

"OK, then, have a nice day!" She tucked the bill on the table and left. Forrest grabbed it before Cimmaron had a chance to, sliding it quickly into his pocket.

"Give that to me!" Cimmaron demanded, thrusting her palm at Forrest. "I pay my own way. I don't let no one do for me, not unless I ask, and I'm not asking."

"I can afford to buy you a glass of iced tea."

"We're not talking what you can or cannot afford—that is *not* the question!"

"Cimmaron—let it go," Jack told her softly. He put his hand on her wrist, and felt the nub of her bracelet under his fingertips. "Just let him do one thing for you. You're probably not going to see each other again, so don't waste your time fighting over stupid stuff. OK? *Let it go.*"

For a moment, Cimmaron seemed confused, as if for the first time since she'd arrived she didn't know exactly how to respond. Finally, with the barest nod, she withdrew her extended hand. "Your one friend has wisdom while your other one has spirit," Cimmaron told Forrest. "I'm glad of that. Me, I barge though life, mostly alone, but it is easier with friends. Good friends. Friends like my Miss Amelia, who is old, but she tells it straight. Those are the ones you keep."

"Yes," Forrest said. "It's only children you give away."

There was a deadly pause as Forrest's words sank in.

Cimmaron hiked her macramé purse to her shoulder as if she were going to leave. Then, seeming to think better of it, let it drop slowly to the ground, the strap slipping through her fingers like sand out of an hourglass. Sighing, she pressed her fingertips into her eyes as she seemed to search for the right words to say. "I came because…I wanted a chance to…explain," she said at last. "I'm sorry, child. Sorry that life can deal us such hard times. You, a mixed child; me, a poor black woman trying to stay alive. I did what I thought I had to do."

"Who was my father?"

Jack was amazed at the dry way Forrest asked the question, as if he were ordering a burger with fries on the side. But his face betrayed him; his lips trembled at the edges.

Cimmaron looked suddenly weary. "He was young, he was handsome—I loved him very much. He died."

Forrest flinched. "Would you tell me something about him? Anything?"

Lips pressed tight, Cimmaron lowered her eyes as if she were peering into the past. In a soft voice she began, "A good man. An American who cared. He was a volunteer for a human rights group that went to Haiti in 1989—"

"To Haiti?" Forrest interrupted.

"Yes. For months he documented the atrocities that

happened there every day, because of the revolution, the poverty, the corruption….Thousands of Haitians were killed by the Macoutes."

"What are Macoutes?" Jack asked.

"Thugs. Criminals. Some of them were soldiers, some police, but all thugs. They roamed in gangs, robbing and murdering." She shook her head. "After so many months of that terror, that constant danger, your father came here, Forrest, to get away from it all, to have a respite for just two short weeks. That was when I met him. I loved him as soon as I saw him."

Ashley sighed because it sounded romantic, but Forrest's face remained expressionless. "What happened next?" he questioned.

"He felt that he had to go back, to gather evidence to tell the world about the atrocities in Haiti. So…I went with him. To help him." She said it as if it were perfectly natural to follow someone into peril. "I knew we would be in terrible danger, because the Macoutes had a list—a hit list—and he was on it. But I wanted to be with him."

The iced tea sat in front of her, untouched. Tracing a finger across the frost on the glass, she continued quietly, "One night the Macoutes dragged him out of the shack. They beat him to death. No one came to help because they were afraid."

"Did—did you see it?" Forrest asked, his voice choked.

A single tear slid down Cimmaron's dark cheek. She brushed it away impatiently as she answered in a bitter voice, "I'd gone to find food for the two of us—food and water were so hard to get. When I came back...." She left the sentence unfinished, but Jack could imagine the scene. It rose unbidden into his imagination: the murdered man, the terrified woman, the horror....

"Others told me that the Macoutes were after me, too. A Haitian family hid me in the slums of Port-au-Prince, but I knew I must escape from the fear, must get back to St. John, because...." She paused and stared directly at Forrest. "Because I was pregnant. With you."

The rest of her words came out in a rush, as though they were so painful she had to tell them quickly or not at all. "Smugglers brought me here to St. John. I had no money, so I signed a paper that I would pay them four thousand dollars as soon as I could. Then you were born...."

Forrest sucked in his breath.

"For a while I couldn't work. The smugglers said if I didn't pay them soon, they would harm you, Forrest. They are terrible, greedy men, as bad as the Macoutes. Maybe worse. Then I found a job as a maid for the Winthrops, but I knew it would be for only a short time because they would be leaving soon—"

"Why didn't you ask them for the money?" Forrest demanded. "They would have given it to you, if you'd only explained."

Cimmaron answered heatedly, "Why should I have burdened them with my troubles? I don't beg for anything from anybody. I work for what I get." A little calmer, she continued, "Mrs. Winthrop—she adored you, Forrest, from the moment she first saw you. When she asked if she could adopt you, I knew you would be safe, because the Winthrops would take you away from harm to where the smugglers couldn't find you. It didn't matter what the smugglers would do to me. I only wanted you to be safe."

Forrest's jaw worked as he stared, not at Cimmaron, but at the street where noisy, laughing students walked in couples or in groups, enjoying their freedom. After a while he murmured, "What is my father's name?"

"Chris. Chris Carter," Cimmaron answered. "He was only 22 when the Macoutes killed him."

"Christopher? Christian?" Forrest urged. "Did he have a middle name? I have to know his exact name so I can find out everything about him. As soon as I get home I'll start a search—"

"No!" Cimmaron was on her feet now. "Forrest, hear me. You have a father. The man who raised you. You belong to those parents, not to me, not to the past. Look forward, never back." Leaning her knuckles against the tabletop, her eyes intent on Forrest's, she said, "You need to be strong. You have the blood of princes in your veins."

Princes? Jack and Ashley exchanged glances. How

could Forrest have the blood of princes if his father had been a young American and his mother was a maid?

Standing tall, Cimmaron said, "I'm leaving now, Forrest. I want you to forget this meeting, forget me."

Forrest exploded, "This can't be good-bye. I'm not done! There's more—I know who you are. I know what you're doing here on St. John."

At those words, Cimmaron froze. The emotion drained from her face. In its place was an expression of polite, detached interest. "I'm a maid. I clean—"

Forrest rocked to his feet. "Forget your excuses. *I know.* Do you understand what I am saying? I have information. Information that can help you. But if you leave now—" When a lady in a pink baseball cap looked over at them, Forrest dropped his voice to a loud whisper. "Why do you think I came on a plane all the way to St. John? It was for you. Not just to find you, but to save you!"

Jack and Ashley stared at one another, wide-eyed. What was Forrest talking about?

"I don't need saving," Cimmaron snapped.

In frustration Forrest jerked his fingers through his hair, leaving faint rows in his tight curls. "Look, the government found out about the operation."

"That is nothing to me. I've done nothing wrong."

"What operation?" Ashley asked, but Forrest went on as though no one else were present.

"All I know is that your name is on a list. An official

from St. John called my father and left the message on his answering machine—as a professional courtesy, the man said. After that I heard your message, too."

"Forrest, what is going on?" Jack demanded. From the tone in Forrest's voice, Jack knew this had to be the secret Forrest wouldn't tell, the one he'd spoken of in their room, the one he'd said had to do with danger.

Jerking her head at Jack and Ashley, Cimmaron asked, "Do they understand?"

"No."

"I ask you to keep it that way."

"Don't worry about Ashley and Jack, worry about the government. You can't do it any more. It's illegal. If you're caught, you'll go to jail."

Cimmaron's mind seemed to be whirring a mile a minute. The tip of her thumbnail made its way into her mouth as she looked out over the harbor. "You said there were names—do you have them?"

The question surprised Forrest. "Yes—I—back at the room," he stammered. "I wrote them down and brought them with me."

"Then I will meet you tonight, in a little park by the wharf. It's called Harbor Park. Be there at seven o'clock tonight. I am a storyteller for the visitors to St. John— no one will think anything if you are there. Bring me the list."

Forrest nodded, and a glimmer of a smile bent the corners of his lips. His mother had fought him, and he had fought back. In a way, that made them equals. And they would meet again, just as Forrest wanted. "Don't worry, I'll be there," he said firmly.

Cimmaron startled Jack by addressing him and his sister. "I know you have no part in this, but hear me." She leaned so close her perfume filled Jack's head. "Lives hang in the balance," she said, her black eyes darting from Jack to Ashley, then back again. "I'm asking you to tell no one what you've just heard. Will you do that for me—for Forrest? For us?"

"But I don't know what it is I'm promising not to tell," Ashley protested. She looked to Jack, who shook his head softly. He didn't know what to do or how to handle this. The words "illegal" and "jail" kept stinging his mind like hornets. Jail was serious, which meant whatever Cimmaron was involved in could be major trouble. They were asking Jack to give his word, and he was someone who kept his promises. Always. It would be better not to commit himself and his sister to covering up anything that sounded like a crime—and yet, was it really covering up if he didn't actually know details? And what about Cimmaron? Did she need protection? Forrest seemed to think so—he'd come all the way to St. John to make sure of it. Were lives really in the balance?

"I don't know...," Jack began reluctantly. It was when he saw Forrest's pleading expression that he caved. Whatever was involved, one thing was certain.

Cimmaron had been about to walk away from Forrest until they'd forged this strange link that was hammered out of names on a list. Somehow Jack knew that if he told, that link between Cimmaron and Forrest would be broken. No, Jack quickly decided, he'd keep quiet. If for nothing else, he'd do it for Forrest.

"Yeah, sure. We won't tell," Jack said. Ashley looked at him, uncertain, before she nodded her agreement.

"All right then." Gentle as a butterfly, Cimmaron bent over Forrest and brushed her lips against his forehead, leaving the faintest blush of red. "You are a good son," she whispered. "When you come tonight, you will hear my stories. I'll tell of a time long before you were born. You will learn of our people. You'll learn of your blood. Tonight, then."

"Yes," Forrest murmured. "Tonight."

They watched as Cimmaron walked down the steps, head high, as though she were a debutante at a ball. Better than a debutante—she climbed into her beat-up old car with its engine that rattled loudly as if she were a queen driving off in a carriage. Forrest's eyes followed her all the way. Then, smiling blissfully, he called for the waitress. Suddenly he was hungry.

Jack couldn't take it any longer. When the waitress left to get Forrest's burger, he blurted, "OK, Ashley and I want to know—what's the list for? Whose names are on it?"

"You heard Cimmaron. The less you know, the

better. If it all blows up, you can say you were innocent." He grinned and took a drag of his Coke, the one the waitress had set down moments before. "But I thank you, Jack. I thank you, Ashley. You don't know what your keeping quiet means to me. You've proven yourselves to be instant and true friends."

Even though she ducked her head to acknowledge the compliment, Ashley looked even less certain than Jack felt. "I've never kept a secret from Mom and Dad," she protested. "Well, OK, maybe I have," she corrected herself. "But not one like this."

"They're going to know something's not right if you act all jumpy. Just behave normally," Forrest coaxed. "Be interested in whatever it is they're talking about. Focus on the conversation. We'll tell them Cimmaron's going to be speaking at the park, and you both need to tell them how much you want to go. I'll do the rest."

"I don't know if I'm any good at acting—" Ashley started to protest, before Forrest cut her off.

"In that case, I'd say you'd better start practicing now. Look across the street by the flagpole. It's your parents. And they're headed our way."

CHAPTER NINE

Jack's parents came into view, waiting for traffic to pass before they darted across the street to the restaurant. Although Olivia wasn't close enough for Jack to read her expression, he could tell by the way she moved that she was worried. Hugging her sides, she hurried after Steven, who marched up the restaurant steps.

"Forrest, are you all right?" Steven asked when he reached them. "Denise told us everything that happened with you and Cimmaron. I'm sorry your mother didn't show up."

"I'm fine, sir. Actually, I'm feeling great. Cimmaron just left."

"She came? Here, to the restaurant?" Olivia asked, incredulous. "But Denise, she said—I thought—"

Forrest smiled broadly, exposing perfect white teeth. "Cimmaron didn't have time to stay, so she wants me to meet her tonight at Harbor Park. She's a storyteller. It's all right if I go, isn't it? Jack and Ashley, too, and you and Mr. Landon, naturally, will be welcome as well. You're excited about coming to hear Cimmaron, aren't you, Ashley?"

He lasered his eyes onto Ashley, who quickly nodded yes.

"And you, Jack?"

Now that his parents were sitting right in front of him, Jack felt uncomfortable with the deception. His parents had raised both him and Ashley to be honest, to be as accountable for the things they chose not to tell as for the things they did. Still, he'd promised Forrest he'd help, and so, mustering as much enthusiasm as he could, he said, "Yeah. Sure. I really want to go."

"So it's all settled. Tonight at Harbor Park."

Exchanging glances with Olivia, Steven told him, "Of course. We'll have to move our plans around a bit, but I'm sure we can get you there, Forrest."

"Plans? What plans?" Ashley asked. "Are we going on a boat ride?"

"No, no, not a boat ride. It's something that could be even better," Steven said. "Your mother will tell you all about it, but let's do first things first. The most important thing you should know, Forrest, is that after several hours on the phone and a truckload of red tape, your parents granted us temporary custody. So, at least for now, you're officially our ward."

"Are they terribly angry?" Forrest's voice was dry and detached, as though nothing concerning his adoptive parents could possibly interest him now.

Steven looked at Forrest quizzically, answering, "They're upset and hurt. When I told them you were here on St. John, they knew immediately that you must have come to trace your birth mother. And, well— they're trying to understand. Your father might not be able to make it, but your mother found a flight that will get her here soon."

"Define soon."

"Tomorrow morning. She'll arrive around ten."

"Do you feel like sharing with us what happened with Cimmaron?" Olivia asked Forrest, trying, it seemed, to pull him back onto the subject of his birth mother. But Forrest answered that he didn't want to talk about Cimmaron, at least not yet, and that his head was too full with worry about what his mother was going to do to him when she arrived from Paris and what he really needed was to talk about other things, since he wanted to get his mind off his troubles. Jack knew it was a dodge; his awareness of that made him shift uneasily. He kept thinking of Cimmaron and the list. Lives hang in the balance. Whose lives? Cimmaron's? Could she be in danger? Or was she the one creating the trouble?

When the waitress reappeared, Forrest made a joke about how she would never be rid of him, at which she giggled and happily supplied Steven and Olivia with menus. Jack wasn't surprised that the waitress was delighted to have Forrest stay. He'd already left her two enormous tips.

While their parents placed their orders, Ashley's eyes met Jack's, and Jack shook his head at her. He could tell by the way his sister's brows crunched together that she was just as worried as he was. As Forrest talked on, his words smooth and wily, Ashley picked up a fork and began to tap it on the edge of the table. *Twink, twink, twink,* like someone plucking a guitar string. *Twink, twink, twink.* When Forrest gave her a look, she slapped the fork onto the table and dropped her hands into her lap.

"Ashley? Jack! What's going on with you two?" Olivia suddenly demanded. "Jack, you keep staring off into space, and Ashley, you're as jumpy as a cat. Are you guys all right?"

"Yeah. Sure. We're fine," Jack mumbled.

"How did your meetings go, Dr. Landon?" Forrest asked, planting his elbows on the table and propping his chin in his hands.

Olivia looked at him with surprise. Jack knew his mother believed in letting kids share at their own pace and in their own time. "Let them be the ones to lead us into things they want to talk about," she'd tell Steven whenever they'd discuss how to bring out a hurting child, one of their "fosters." Jack watched now as his mother shifted mental gears.

"Well, Forrest, the seminar was intense. Disturbing, of course, to learn how badly damaged the coral reefs have become. Are you sure you want to talk about this? I mean, now?"

"Absolutely. I'm really very interested. Didn't you say the reefs are actually living creatures?" Forrest pressed, pretending an interest but figuring, Jack knew, that it would be a good way to turn the conversation in a completely different direction. You had to hand it to Forrest, Jack thought. He was as cool and calculating as any diplomat could be.

"Yes, that's the reason I came to St. John—we're studying ways to save the reefs," Olivia said, smiling at him. There was nothing she liked better than to explain science to an audience of kids, even if, as in this case, her own kids counted for two-thirds of the audience. If Forrest wanted to hear, Olivia wouldn't disappoint.

"You're in for it now, Forrest," Steven joked. Olivia gave Steven a playful punch and replied, "If they're coming with us tonight, they should know this stuff."

"True," Steven agreed.

"Coral reefs are one of nature's most magnificent creations," she began, turning her attention back to the three of them. "They've been around for about 400 million years. They're similar to rain forests in that they provide homes for many different creatures—hundreds of species of fish, crabs, lobsters, starfish, sea urchins, sea cucumbers, anemones...." She was ticking them off on her fingers while she spoke. "So when the reefs are destroyed, a lot of creatures become homeless, and today too many reefs are being destroyed. We have already lost one-tenth of the world's coral reefs—can you believe that?" Her voice rose in indignation. "One-tenth! Another third will probably be lost in the next 20 years—even without climate change. They get damaged from pollution, sewage, and other debris dumped into coastal waters—things like fish lines and nets and plastic bottles and garbage. People can be so careless!"

"Or maybe they're just uncaring," Steven broke in. "Or ignorant. When swimmers stand on reefs or boaters drop anchors there, they crush and break coral. Because coral grows only about an inch a year, it takes a very long time to recover from that kind of human-caused destruction."

Taking over again, Olivia said, "At the meeting, I was talking to an expert on coral reefs—her name is Ginger Garrison. When I told her about all that anchor damage we saw this morning at Jumbie Bay, she was really surprised. She said she couldn't imagine why anyone would be dropping anchor there—it's just not a place where boaters ever stop. You know, coral isn't just rock; it's made up of tiny, fragile, living animals called coral polyps...."

As his parents went on with their explanation, Jack kept wondering at Forrest's cool demeanor. Tonight he was going to pass off a list of names, like a spy, and yet he could change his face into a mask that hid every-thing going on inside him. He kept his eyes locked on Olivia's, as if he didn't want to miss a single word, even when the waitress brought their salads and refilled the glasses of iced tea. Steven, whose pale skin was already turning pink on the top of his head from the heat, gulped his gratefully, but Olivia left hers untouched. She was as interested in sharing the story of the reefs as Forrest pretended to be in hearing it.

"What about global warming?" Forrest asked. "I read an article that said global warming is maybe the biggest danger to reefs. Is that correct?"

"That's absolutely right, Forrest," Olivia said, look-ing impressed. "Just a two-degree rise in maximum water temperature can stress corals, even kill them. And that's what's been happening all over the world because of global warming."

Jack was puzzled. Even though he was only half listening, the gloom and doom his mother was report-ing about the dying coral reefs should have been a real downer, yet Jack saw a spark in her eyes, an under-current that didn't match the words she spoke. There was something else going on. Knowing how his mother operated, he figured she'd lead up to it through a lot of layers of talk before she'd spring the surprise on them, if that's what that half-hidden excitement meant—a surprise. Something good.

"Among reef creatures that have already been

harmed," she continued, "are sea turtles. One species is not only endangered, it's *critically* endangered, which is even worse—and that's the hawksbill turtle, the kind we were lucky enough to see at Jumbie Bay this morning. Like other sea dwellers, hawksbills need coral reefs—"

"Oh, go ahead and tell them," Steven broke in, grinning at Olivia. "You can fill them in on the details about hawksbills on our way to the beach tonight."

"Beach? Tonight?" Ashley sat up straight, her brown eyes darting from her father to her mother and back.

"Yes. We'll go back to Jumbie Bay after our time at Harbor Park," Olivia informed them. "At the meeting, I heard that a hawksbill turtle was seen nesting—laying her eggs—on the beach at Jumbie Bay last night. Maybe she's the turtle we saw this morning, but there's a chance that another one or two might come to lay eggs tonight. It'll be a perfect night to watch them—a full moon, mild weather...."

"But I can still go to see Cimmaron, right?" Forrest interrupted. For the first time, Jack heard tension in his voice. The mask had slipped just a little.

"Yes. There's no reason we can't do both," Olivia told him. "First the park, then the beach. If we're lucky enough to watch turtles laying eggs, you won't be sorry. It really would be an incredible experience!"

"Right. Incredible." Forrest didn't sound convincing at all, and Jack worried that his parents would notice.

"It's all right, Forrest," Olivia said, covering his hand with hers. "We'll get you to the park. You'll see Cimmaron again."

#

Since they expected to have a late night, it was decided they should all take naps, which suited Forrest fine because that meant they'd return to the motel. Once inside the small box of a room, Forrest kicked off his shoes and sprawled onto his bed, rolling onto his back so that his head rested in his hands. Jack sat on the edge of his own lumpy mattress, waiting for some sort of explanation. It wasn't long before Forrest said, "You've been great, Jack. Ashley was a little nervous, but I don't think your folks caught on. I tried to keep the conversation on the coral reefs, but to be honest, I hardly tracked what your mother was saying. Even though I think I asked the right questions, I kept imagining she could see inside my head and know that my mind was a million miles away. So, how did I do?"

Before Jack could answer, there was a soft knock on the door. When he opened it, Ashley hurried inside and jumped up to sit crossed-legged on Jack's bed.

"I don't think I want to keep your secret anymore, Forrest. I mean, I'm not sure what to think about any of this," she announced, just like that. "All the time Mom was talking about the hawksbill turtle and the coral reef, I kept remembering Cimmaron and jail and all the stuff you were saying to each other. Forrest, what's going on?"

For such a small person, Ashley could take up a lot of space. Her hair, which usually hung in smooth ringlets, now curled wildly because of the humidity; she had placed her elbows on her knees as if she were a pyramid of joints and angles, and she was leaning forward, expectantly.

Jack dropped down next to his sister and nodded in agreement. "Ashley's right," he said. "Cimmaron said that lives hang in the balance. I know what I promised, but I'm not sure we should keep quiet." Jack swallowed the last words, because he never broke his word if he could help it. But this thing had become bigger than any promise; if something went wrong, if someone died, Jack and Ashley would be a part of it. Somehow, between the Songbird restaurant and the motel, Jack's mind had become clear. It was too big a price.

Forrest pushed himself up and faced them. His bicep bulged as he rested on one elbow.

"You're right. I should tell you everything I know— I owe you that much. After that you can decide what to do." He blew a breath between his teeth, then rolled off the bed, padding over to his duffel bag, which had been shoved into the corner. Unzipping the front pocket, he began to carefully remove layers of clothing. "I need to start at the beginning when I heard the message. No...." He stopped, looked at them for a moment, remembering. "I'll begin farther back than that. I took a cab from my boarding school to our Denver home.

I wanted to get some soccer equipment that I'd left in my basement. Of course, I'm not supposed to leave the school campus without permission, but I simply called a cab and left. I have a key to my house."

He rifled through the duffel before pulling out a folded piece of paper. "After I'd found my equipment, I stopped in my dad's den. It's magnificent—lots of mahogany and Tiffany lamps. His office has always been off limits to me because it is full of his private, important things, but I figured just this once, since he was in France....In any event, the message light on his phone was blinking. I decided to play it. That's when I heard."

Unfolding the paper, he placed it in Jack's hands. Three names were written down, two men's and one woman's: *Bené Phillipe, Arlen Smith, and Cimmaron* had been carefully transcribed in Forrest's precise script.

"The man leaving the message was some official from the Virgin Islands. He said there was going to be an investigation on St. John, that they were planning to arrest everyone on the list and that he wanted to let my father know Cimmaron was one of them. He said he remembered that Cimmaron was the mother of his adopted son, and he kept saying that he was uncomfortable apprehending her but that he'd have to if she was working with the others. He told my father he hoped by giving him a 'heads-up,' he could prevent something embarrassing. 'Professional courtesy,' he said." As Forrest practically spat the word "courtesy," Jack felt Ashley wince.

"You've got to understand—my parents have never given me any information about my birth mother except her name. Nothing about who she was or how they met her or why she let them adopt me."

"I still don't get it—what were the people on the list doing?" Ashley asked.

Forrest pressed his lips together, making a grim line. "I honestly don't know. The message said it was illegal. Cimmaron would get arrested. I had to warn her."

Jack shook his head. "How can you protect her when you don't know what she's into? What if it's drugs?"

"Don't you think I've thought of that?" Forrest flared. "But she's my mother! She's my blood! My 'parents' have held back the truth from me—I don't know what to believe anymore." Pacing, Forrest walked a tight circle at the end of the bed. "You met her. Do you honestly think Cimmaron would be a part of anything evil? Do you really want her to go to jail?"

"No," Ashley began, "but—"

"Let me do this for her. Please!" Forrest begged. "Don't stop me."

Ashley and Jack looked helplessly at one another. How much truth did they owe their parents? How much loyalty did they owe Forrest, whom they hadn't even known a day and a half ago?

Jack couldn't answer that.

CHAPTER TEN

Harbor Park was only a football-field-size patch of grass, cut through with sidewalks and surrounded by older, flat-faced buildings. The south side of the park, which was where the Landons stood now, abruptly ended at the bay. Jack noticed that the water was murky-brown instead of jewel-colored like the waters of Jumbie Bay, and he wondered at the difference those few miles made. Steven explained that the harbor had been dredged so that ships could come in, which made it much deeper and therefore darker.

Overhead, seagulls screeched, as if in answer to a tugboat that blew its whistle in the distance. A colorful assortment of people streamed past, people of all shades. Everyone seemed happy—joking, laughing, even singing right out loud. Jack would have liked to watch the ships, to drink in the salty smell of the water and take in the carnival atmosphere, but there was no way he could stand still for more than a moment, at least not while Forrest was with them. Since the park wasn't far from their motel, they'd decided to walk, which had been a mistake. Forrest never stopped pressing them forward, pushing and prodding like a sheepdog herding its flock. "Let's go!" he urged. "Cimmaron's waiting!"

"Forrest, chill. It's not time for her to start yet," Ashley said.

"I know, but I need to get a good seat."

"That's not going to be a problem," Jack retorted. "Look—no one's even in the park." That was true. Most people walking along the park's sidewalks seemed to be passing through in order to get to one restaurant or another that ringed its edge. A few middle-aged couples sauntered toward a café decorated with white Christmas lights, while younger ones were headed to an open-fronted bar where a steel band played loudly. Most of the park benches stood empty.

"Do you even see Cimmaron?" Olivia asked him.

Forrest shielded his eyes, a worried expression on his face. Excitedly, he pointed to the opposite end. "That must be her, over there. Look at all those kids!"

In the distance Jack could see a cluster of children sitting cross-legged on the grass. One girl turned cartwheels, her long legs and arms at right angles as she spun up and down, up and down, like a pinwheel.

Cimmaron sat on a bench in front of the group, her head bent back in laughter. "I'm going to her," Forrest announced. He began to run, leaving the Landons to watch his retreating figure.

"Bye, Forrest," Ashley called to his back.

Steven sighed. "You can't blame him for being eager. This whole thing has got to be pretty hard on him. When I was a kid being bounced around from one foster home to another, I used to dream I had a mother out there, somewhere in the world. I'd pretend that finding her would make my life perfect, but of course for me it never happened. In a way, it's happening for Forrest."

"The difference is that Forrest already has a mother," Jack reminded him. "And a father. How did they sound on the phone?"

"Like I told you before, his father seemed genuinely concerned about Forrest's happiness. I was impressed with him." He stopped walking now, and Olivia stood still as well. "What did you two think of Cimmaron?"

At the question, Ashley shot Jack a look, then locked her eyes on the ground. She seemed suddenly fascinated with a grubby seagull feather, moving it back and forth along the path with her toe. How, Jack wondered, could he answer that without lying? Taking a pair of mental scissors, Jack cut out the parts of Cimmaron that might reveal too much; he ended up with a short list of her qualities, the number one being "proud."

"Good," Steven said, moving again. "I'm sure she

has a lot to be proud of. Forrest seems like a great kid."

"Hey, look over there," Ashley cried, pointing to the building where a drum beat wildly. "Isn't that Denise?"

A set of double doors stood wide open, allowing both music and light to radiate from within. Denise, who had traded her park uniform for a coral sheath, moved fluidly around the small dance floor, while her partner, a tall, muscular black man, pivoted rhythmically to match her every move. The two of them seemed to be having a marvelous time. They looked like a poster for everything that was appealing about St. John.

"Should we go say hi?" Ashley asked.

Olivia shook her head no. "Let's give the poor woman a break. She's already put in a full day with the Landon crew."

Strolling leisurely, they made their way toward Forrest. He was sitting on the bench next to his mother, his head close to hers, deep in conversation. He must have already given her the list because she held a piece of paper in her hand. So he'd done it. Now Forrest had become part of whatever it was Cimmaron was involved with. A dark taste rose in Jack's mouth as he watched Cimmaron fold the paper small and drop it into her purse. Once again he thought of telling his parents about the mysterious list of names. No, he knew before the thought was half-formed he couldn't do it. This had become way too important to Forrest.

In a flash, Jack saw clearly that it didn't matter that

he didn't have the money Forrest had or the fancy education. Jack had a great family, one without any complicated history, who got along with each other most of the time and who laughed at the same jokes. Who could guess how Jack would have turned out if his life had been different? It was possible that he might have been just as demanding as Forrest. Maybe worse. As Jack approached the park bench, he suddenly felt grateful for his more ordinary existence. He wouldn't trade places for anything.

"Well, we meet again," Cimmaron said, nodding to Jack and Ashley. "You must be the Landons." Rising to her feet, she extended her hand to Steven, then Olivia. "I want to thank you for taking care of Forrest. He told me what you did for him."

"I'm glad this has turned out so well. Forrest says you're a storyteller," Olivia said.

"Yes, I tell the stories about my people, stories of where we came from. I'm almost ready to tell the children. Would you like to join them?"

Jack looked at the group of wiggling children, who ranged in age from four to twelve. An older girl had a baby slung on her hip, its dark hair parted in cornrows shaped like lightning bolts. It was almost seven o'clock, and as if on cue, the group gathered at Cimmaron's feet, jostling to see who could get closest. Forrest stayed by Cimmaron's side, beaming at the small crowd. After his latest shower, he'd put on khaki pants, pressed with a knife pleat, and a purple polo shirt. He'd stayed in the bathroom almost an hour getting ready and emerged looking as though each curl had been individually formed. He looked perfect.

"Do you mind sitting on the grass, Dr. Landon?" Forrest asked.

"Me? No, that's fine," Olivia told him. She settled next to Steven, leaning her head back on his shoulder. What was it about St. John that made people act so romantic? Jack dropped down beside his father. Ashley was on his right.

As Cimmaron gathered her thoughts to begin, Ashley asked softly, "Did Forrest...?"

"Yes," Jack answered. "I saw her holding it."

Ashley didn't say any more, but she chewed the edge of her lip, a sure sign she felt worried.

"Ladies and gentlemen, boys and girls," Cimmaron boomed, "I bid you welcome. Before I tell the story of our past, I must introduce you to someone very special. This is Forrest, a boy from Colorado and the city of Denver. He will sit by my side while I tell the stories."

Cimmaron put her hands on her knees, and Forrest quickly did the same. Chin high, Forrest looked out over the knot of children, swelling with pride as Cimmaron began the story of her people's island history.

Many, many years ago, at the beginning of the 18th century—yes, way back then—the island was called

St. Jan, part of the Danish West Indies. White planters grew cotton, but the main crop was sugarcane, sugar to make rum, to bring wealth to the island. Did any white planter ever work in the cane fields? Never! That was slave work. Slaves planted the sugarcane, chopped it with machetes, and squeezed it into rum. The only trade that brought in greater wealth than rum was the buying and selling of slaves.

Not only white people owned slaves. No. It grieves me to say that in the black homeland, all over Africa, one tribe would make a raid on another tribe. Warriors would capture a few or a dozen enemies and turn them into slaves.

Sometimes those enemies who were captured and sold into slavery had been princes in their own tribes or even kings. These were proud, handsome warriors who had never done such lowly work as digging or planting, because those jobs were women's work.

Hundreds of slaves—men, women, and children—were crowded onto ships and borne across the seas. If they survived the brutal voyage across the Atlantic Ocean to the Caribbean Sea—and far too many did not—they would be stood up on the auction block in St. Thomas. Auction day was a rare treat for the island's citizens. Free and slave alike, all the island people would crowd the marketplace where the frightened slaves, who did not understand a word of the strange languages they heard, were sold to the highest bidders.

For the islanders, who had little in the way of entertainment, a slave auction was like a holiday.

The docile captives, the ones who kept their heads down to hide their tears of despair, were prodded to walk forward and backward and to raise their arms high, so that prospective buyers could judge whether their bodies were strong and healthy enough to perform the brutally hard work. The prouder, angry captives—the ones of royal blood who had owned slaves of their own in Africa—were chained to the rails and beaten with whips. Too often, the smoldering rage that seethed from their eyes and their clenched fists would discourage planters from bidding high prices for them.

In 1732, two Africans of royal blood, one a king of the Adampe tribe and the other a prince of the Aquambo tribe, were taken to St. Jan in manacles and leg irons, chained night and day so they would not run away. One thousand slaves lived on the island of St. Jan, all of them owned by only 200 white planters.

For the planters on St. Jan, that year—1732—was the worse they'd ever known. A terrible drought seared the fruits on the trees and shrank the vegetables in the ground. Water barrels stood empty for so long their wooden staves dried out and split. When at last a little rain fell, it moistened the ground only enough for a plague of grasshoppers to arise. When the grasshoppers had eaten everything left above ground, a plague of caterpillars consumed everything below the ground.

The slaves were starving. As if their suffering were not already unbearable, a terrible hurricane struck the island, ripping away roofs, flattening walls, sinking boats in the harbors and sweeping donkeys and goats and roosters out to sea.

There was nothing left to eat, because everything had been destroyed. "Work harder!" the overseers cried, slashing their whips across the naked backs of the slaves, backs already scarred by crisscross welts. One by one the slaves began to slip away from the plantations, hiding in the bush under cover of darkness, in the wild, overgrown thickness through which no white man could find his way.

At night the drums sounded, sending messages from one end of the island to the other. The sound of the drums guided the runaways, who were called "marons"—the word "maron" coming from "Cimmaron," meaning "wild and unruly and free."

Cimmaron paused to allow her audience to make the connection. As they did, a ripple of murmurs swept through the children. Then she continued.

Always the drums told the marons where to come, where to hide. The prince of the Aquambo tribe and the king of the Adampe tribe were among the first to escape from their masters. Those two men were sworn enemies, but their hatred of their masters and their yearning for freedom united them. When they met in the bush, the king and the prince banded together with other slaves to lead a revolt. They believed that every slave on the island of St. Jan would join them in their revolt. They believed they could drive all the white people from St. Jan. When that was done, they believed they would rule St. Jan as their own kingdom.

At night, the drums never stopped beating their message. At three in the morning on November 23, 1733, the sound of drums was swallowed by the boom of cannon. The rebels had captured the garrison at Coral Bay, where they killed all the Danish soldiers. Then, slowly, swiftly, secretly, the rebels slipped into the houses of the planters and killed the ones who could not escape. They ordered household slaves and field slaves to join them in the revolt, until their ranks swelled, but only into the hundreds because many of the slaves stayed loyal to their white masters.

Months passed, and each night the drums thundered, sending messages from one rebel stronghold to the next. Then, because France and Denmark were allies, French ships arrived from the island of Martinique, bearing hundreds of highly trained French soldiers with guns.

Soon the rebels saw that their cause was hopeless. As the French soldiers advanced on them, shooting them, hanging them, and beheading them, the rebels decided they would rather be dead than be slaves again. Some leaped to their deaths, falling from a cliff to the rocks below. Others shot themselves with guns

*captured from the soldiers. Among those who com-
mitted suicide was the king of the Adampes.*

*The prince of the Aquambo and his followers still
hid in the bush. By then, there were so few slaves left
that the governor decided to pardon the remaining
rebels, providing they promised to return to work on
the plantations. When the drums sent this message to
the prince, he led his ragged band of followers onto the
estate where he had once worked like a woman in
the fields. He knew the revolt had failed, but he trusted
the governor to pardon him, as had been promised.*

*As the prince of the Aquambo walked toward the
place of surrender, his head held high even in defeat,
a sergeant of the Danish guard took aim and shot him.
The prince fell, his life's blood flowing out onto the
ground that had never been his.*

*But months before his death, the prince had fathered
a baby girl. She was born in the bush, and he named her
Princess Alia. That baby girl grew up strong and proud
like her father. She was a princess of the Aquambo, here
on St. Jan, and she became mother to my grandmother's
grandmother's grandmother's grandmother.*

For a long moment all the sounds of boat horns, of
people chatting, of music blaring from the restaurants
seemed to fade. Nothing remained except the drama
of Cimmaron's final words. Then, softly, Forrest asked,
"So you and I are descended from an African prince?"

"We are, indeed," Cimmaron replied. "You are a prince. Of royal blood. Never forget that." As she stood, tall and regal, Jack could almost imagine a crown on her head, except an African princess wouldn't have worn a crown.

The story was still resonating inside Jack's head, filling it with dark images, when Cimmaron announced, "It was good to meet you all, but now I must go."

"But I thought we could have more time!" Forrest protested, clutching her hand.

"Actually, we're on our way hoping to see a hawksbill turtle nesting, and you're welcome to join us," Steven offered.

"No, I must leave. But I'll see you again, Forrest."

Forrest's eyes narrowed as he asked, "When? How?"

"Soon. Don't detain me now. Remember, I told you I have an important job to do." Her eyes bore into Forrest, who nodded reluctantly. "Goodbye, Dr. Landon. Mr. Landon," she said, shaking their hands. "Ashley, Jack, I'm sorry to go so suddenly. I will call in the morning, Forrest, and we can decide more. Until tomorrow."

As suddenly as Cinderella leaving the ball, Cimmaron gave a final wave to the children and disappeared down the sidewalk. Forrest watched her retreating figure.

"Forrest," Olivia said gently, "are you all right?"

"Don't worry about me," he answered, his voice strangely steady. "Didn't you hear what she said about the people I came from? I can deal with anything."

CHAPTER ELEVEN

"It was nice of Denise to let us use her Jeep tonight," Ashley said.

"It isn't Denise's Jeep. It belongs to the Park Service, and Mom's here on park business," Jack reminded her. "But yeah, Denise is nice. Very cool lady. You ought to be more like her."

"What do you mean? What's wrong with the way I am?" Ashley demanded.

"Oh, only everything," Jack teased.

Ashley reached across Forrest to punch Jack. Forrest didn't react, not even when Ashley's and Jack's arms crisscrossed him and got all jumbled up as they escalated into a mock battle. Forrest seemed to have sunk deeply into his own worries, frowning, his lips moving as though he were arguing with himself.

"Don't fight back there, you two," Steven ordered.

"I don't need the distraction. I'm having a hard enough time remembering to drive on the wrong side of the road." Although a full moon had begun to rise over the rim of the island, the twisting North Shore Road was only dimly lighted, creating a tangle of moon shadows on the surface. Steven's hands gripped the wheel.

"It's not the wrong side of the road for the people of St. John," Jack answered. "If they came to Wyoming, they'd think *we* were driving on the wrong side."

Olivia turned to face the kids in the back seat, pointing a warning finger first at Jack and then at Ashley, a wordless signal that meant, "Settle down." Which they did, after rolling their eyes at one another.

"You need to realize that seeing a hawksbill nesting is a rare treat." Olivia told them. "The numbers of hawksbills has declined drastically. It's not just that their habitats are being destroyed because the coral reefs are dying. There's an even bigger threat: Poaching."

"Poaching?" Forrest asked, frowning. "You mean like poached eggs?"

Jack couldn't help himself—he hooted. So Forrest IV didn't know everything after all, in spite of his expensive education! He thought "poached" meant an alternative to fried or scrambled. "Poaching," Jack explained when he could stop laughing, "is like when Robin Hood and his Merry Men hunted deer on the king's lands. They were taking something illegally—hunting in a place they weren't allowed to."

"And poaching is especially bad," Ashley chimed in, "when people steal species that are endangered."

Poor Forrest, he must have felt bombarded because right then Olivia went into her lecture mode. "It's bad enough when poachers steal the turtle eggs," she said. "Even though buying and selling them are illegal, there are, unfortunately, a lot of people who like to eat those eggs. What's worse is when poachers take female hawksbills right off the beach while they're trying to nest. Once female turtles start laying eggs, they'll stay in one place for an hour or two until they're finished, so they're really vulnerable. It's easy to capture them then."

"What do poachers steal them for?" Forrest asked. "Turtle soup?"

"Mmm, that too, but it's only a very small part of their value. It's the hawksbills' carapaces that poachers want," Olivia told him. "In other words, the turtles' shells. Tortoiseshell. It gets made into jewelry and eyeglass frames and earrings and such, and it sells on the black market for $50 to $60 per pound. In Japan, as much as $100 a pound."

"That's not so much money," Forrest murmured.

"It is for some people. And as hawksbills get more scarce, the price of their shells just keeps rising."

"My mother has—" Forrest began, then stopped.

Jack figured he'd been about to say that his mother owned tortoiseshell earrings or glasses frames or whatever, then decided not to.

Or maybe Forrest stopped because just at that moment, an old blue Chevy passed them on the right and raced into the night. Jack caught only a glimpse of the back of the driver's head—lots of hair, wild and unruly. Cimmaron? Maybe Forrest had seen the driver's face as she roared past.

Steven said, "We'll take a flashlight so we can find our way down to Jumbie Beach, but once we get there we have to turn it off. Lights make turtles disoriented. If they see artificial lights, they turn around and go back into the ocean without laying their eggs."

"There's a big moon up there," Ashley pointed out. "We might not even need a flashlight."

"We'll take it anyway. Once the turtle is done nesting, we can use the light. It won't bother her then. Now, you guys start checking for mile marker 3. That's where we're supposed to pull off and park."

Almost before he'd finished saying that, Ashley shouted, "There it is. Mile marker 3."

Steven swerved the Jeep into a small parking area at the side of the road and turned off the motor. After they piled out of the Jeep, they used their flashlight to guide them down the wooden steps to Jumbie Beach. When Jack saw the moonlight reflecting in the water of Jumbie Bay, it looked so inviting that he wanted to rip off his sandals and run splashing into the surf.

"OK everyone, stay back," his mother warned. "We're only going to the edge of these trees. We don't want to scare away any turtles that might show up."

"What if the turtles don't come?" Ashley asked. "How long are we going to wait to see if they get here? If they don't come, can we go wading?"

"Not tonight," Steven told her. "Tomorrow I'll take all of you snorkeling at Trunk Bay, where there's a wonderful coral reef. No matter what happens here tonight, we'll go to Trunk Bay tomorrow—promise!"

Ashley sighed loudly, then hunkered down at the foot of a tree where shadows would hide her from any approaching turtles. Forrest moved a little apart from the family, still absorbed in his own worries. Crouching down, he became part of the tree line. Jack thought about sitting near him, then decided Forrest wanted to be alone. His parents seemed to sense it as well, since they didn't pry. They let Forrest know where they were, then left him to his own thoughts.

It wasn't a bad way to spend a couple of hours, Jack decided. Water lapped the sandy beach, the moon continued to glide through a dark sky punctuated with constellations, and the bugs weren't too bothersome—although Ashley always attracted a lot more bugs than Jack did. He could hear her slapping her arms in the dark until their mother whispered for her to be still.

The night couldn't have been any quieter, no sounds but the water sliding onto shore and sliding back, and the call of a single night bird who didn't seem to know it was bedtime. That, plus a bit of rustling that Jack couldn't identify. It seemed to come first from one side of him, then the other, then from behind, as though some animal were circling through the brush.

Ashley leaned close to him, whispering, "Did you hear that? It's the Jumbies. This is their beach."

"Don't be dumb," Jack whispered back. "It's probably a couple of mongooses looking for people to bite."

"Well, thanks!" she said half aloud. "That makes me feel a whole lot better!"

"Shhh!" Olivia hissed.

Jack kept straining his eyes to look for turtles. Even though he was just inside the tree line, he had a good view of the beach. The part right ahead of him was pure, clean sand, smoothed by the waves, but to the left of that, a number of good-size rocks lined the shore. When he stared at them glistening in the moonlight as the waves surged forward, he could almost convince himself that the rocks were moving. A couple of times he thought one of them might be a turtle, but he knew turtles wouldn't emerge on the rocky part of the beach— they needed open sand where they could dig their nests.

Ashley stretched her arms over her head so high that her shoulders popped in their sockets. Leaning over, she murmured, "How long have we been here?"

Jack glanced at the luminescent dial on the face of his watch. "Two hours and six minutes."

"My bottom hurts. I think it's gone completely numb. Do you think Forrest is OK?" she whispered.

"Yeah. He just wants to be alone."

"You're all right with Forrest's...you know...."

Although it was dark, Jack understood what she was asking. Was he OK about Forrest's list? "Yes," he answered at last. "I guess it'll all work out. We don't really know what she's up to, so none of it's our fault, right?"

"Right," Ashley agreed. She didn't sound convinced.

Suddenly he felt Ashley's hand, clawlike, on his arm. Silently, she pointed to a serpentine head held high out of the surf. A turtle! Lumbering slowly, clumsily, it emerged from the surf to make its way up onto the beach, leaving turtle tracks in the sand.

"It's a hawksbill," Olivia whispered. "I can't believe it...I was hoping, but...here it is!"

"Shhh!" Ashley whispered fiercely, happy, it seemed, to shush her mother for once. But then she added, "I wonder if it's our turtle from this morning."

Halfway between the edge of the water and the trees where the Landons were hiding, the turtle stopped. For a long while it sat on the sand, as though considering whether this would be a good spot to dig a nest.

Jack could see his father changing the setting on his camera—opening the shutter wide so he could take pictures without flash. Any bright light at that moment would have disturbed the turtle enough that she'd turn around and hurry back into the sea—as much as any turtle could hurry.

Slowly, using flippers that looked as long and curved as angel wings, she flung away loose sand. Then, digging with her flippers and rotating her body, she began to hollow out a pit. Time must have been passing because the moon had moved overhead, but the nesting fascinated Jack so much that he could have stayed completely still and watched all night. There were no sounds except the quiet clicking of the shutter as Steven took pictures and the grunting of the turtle as she began to lay her eggs in the pit—plus the rustling that could have been the mongooses.

Then Jack heard a gasp from Forrest, and on the other side of him, an echoing gasp from his sister. Both of them were staring at the waters of Jumbie Bay, where a 20-foot wooden boat drifted silently toward the shore. The front of the boat was crowded with human figures, silhouetted in the moonlight.

"Jumbies," Ashley cried in fright.

"Quiet!" Steven told her softly. "It's probably just some fishermen, or it could be tourists. Maybe they're looking for turtles, too. Just watch and wait."

Like a ghost ship, the boat drew closer and closer until it came to rest about 20 feet from shore, where it dropped anchor. Half a dozen dark shapes leaped out of the boat and started toward the shore. If they were ghosts, they should have glided soundlessly across the surface of the water; instead, they splashed noisily through the surf until they reached the beach. Then, calling softly in a language Jack didn't know, they began to run across the sand—right toward the Landons!

"Poachers!" Steven cried under his breath. But the dark shadows paid no attention to the nesting turtle; instead they ran straight for the trees, disappearing into the inky blackness, shadows into shadow.

"What should we do—where's the flashlight?" Olivia cried. In the darkness, as Steven fumbled to connect his flash attachment to his camera, four more dark shapes ran past them, melting into the trees.

Two other people—both men—had jumped out of the boat and were heading straight for the turtle. "Give me a hand with this—it's heavy," one man said, as he tried to get a hold on one end of the turtle's shell.

"What 'bout dem eggs?" the other man asked, his voice carrying clearly in the night.

"We'll get them next. I love the smell of turtle— smells just like money!"

The men grunted as they lifted the turtle as high as their knees. With bowed backs, they began to make their way toward their wooden vessel.

"They're taking her! No way—stop! Leave her here!" Olivia shouted, leaping up from the blanket.

"Mom, wait! They might have guns!" Ashley screamed. In a flash she was beside her mother, with Steven right behind both of them, grabbing Olivia's arm.

Wrenching her arm free, Olivia cried, "We can't just watch—they'll kill her for the shell!"

Alerted by her cries, the poachers started to run. Curses rained down as they splashed toward the boat, the turtle swinging wildly between them. Jack knew this turtle would die. If the men threw her on the boat, they would wrench the shell from her back and kill her and all the eggs she was still carrying. Taking a step forward, he felt the flashlight beneath his shoe. The light. If he could catch them in the flashlight's beam, he'd be able to see the registration number on the boat and give it to the authorities. In an instant he scooped up the flashlight and fumbled for the switch. His hands felt as stiff as if they'd been held under cold water—why wouldn't his fingers work right? The flashlight tumbled from his hands to the ground, but when he grabbed it once more and commanded himself to calm down, he located the switch and turned it on.

The beam cut the night like a saber. He knew the poachers would flee like cockroaches rather than let anyone get a good look at their faces. But the moment he tried to aim the beam at them, he felt something hit him from behind.

"What!?!" Jack stammered. He took a step but found himself reeling—a poacher must have found him, knocking him onto his back. He felt a vise-like grip as a hand attempted to pry the flashlight from his fingers. Then Jack caught a flash of a face in the beam. Forrest. It was Forrest, trying with all his might to wrestle the light away.

"Give...it...to...me!" Forest said between gritted teeth. He was strong, but Jack punched him with an elbow, rolling free in the cool sand. Forrest fell onto his back but was up on his feet as fast as lighting, lunging once again at Jack. *"Give it up!"* he grunted. Driving at Jack's middle, he pushed him to the ground, landing on top of him with a thud. They flipped, one over the other, and Jack felt his flesh scraping against tree root. Forrest had gone crazy. Nothing made sense.

As Jack fought back, the beam of the flashlight bounced crazily through the trees where a half dozen dark forms were running straight up the rocky hillside toward North Shore Road. In that wildly swinging beam of light, Jack saw one face that he recognized before Forrest knocked the light out of his hand. Cimmaron!

Suddenly everything was happening at once—the poachers calling down more curses as they frantically splashed toward the boat; Steven firing off one camera shot after another at the poachers' retreating figures; Forrest rolling onto his back, panting, the fight over; a siren sounding in the bay with a teeth-grinding wail. When another boat chugged toward shore, shining a huge spotlight that caught the men full in its beam, the two men dropped the turtle. People jumped out of this boat, too, churning up the water as they made their way toward the poachers, who slowly raised their hands in surrender. Every one of the people from the second boat was in uniform.

"Hands up!" blared a voice from a bullhorn. "Do *not* reach for a weapon! Keep your hands in the air!"

"Thank heavens," Olivia cried. "They must be from the U.S. Fish and Wildlife Service. They've come to catch the poachers. Jack! Where's Jack?" she suddenly cried, looking wildly around. "Forrest?"

"We're here," Jack called out. She couldn't see them under the trees, but hearing Jack's voice must have been enough. Once again she ran forward with Steven right behind her, reaching the soaked, angry poachers just as the officers snapped handcuffs on them.

So that's what the list was all about! Jack realized. Cimmaron was involved with men who poached turtles! It was despicable. No wonder Forrest had wanted to keep anyone from recognizing Cimmaron—she was part of the worst kind of crime. Forrest lay on his back, panting, his knees wet with sand; Jack was next to him, too spent to move. The flashlight lay between them, its beam lighting the gnarled roots of a tamarind tree.

"You saw, didn't you?" Forrest rasped.

"Yeah, I saw," Jack said, rubbing a spot on his cheek that burned.

"Jack…I'm sorry…."

"Yeah. Whatever." Rolling to his feet, he brushed himself off and smoothed his hair, then made his way to where his parents were standing.

"…relieved you caught them!" Olivia was exclaiming to the officers. "We were here watching the hawksbill nest and then these men came and tried to steal it."

"Whoa, slow down, lady. Who are you?" the officer asked. "And who's this guy with you, and what are kids doing out here?"

It took a good four or five minutes for Olivia and Steven to explain why they were on Jumbie Beach. Luckily, Olivia had identification in her wallet that proved who she was and why she happened to be in St. John as a guest of the Park Service. Again, Jack had the feeling that all this drama was taking place on stage, maybe because the huge, unrelenting spotlight from the officers' boat was shining right at all of them.

"I got plenty of shots of those two turtle poachers," Steven told the officers. "I caught them in the act with my camera. You'll have the pictures as evidence when you prosecute them."

"That'll help put them away, but it's not what we're arresting them for," one of the officers told Steven.

Steven's frown was accentuated by the bright light from the boat. "You're not? But we saw them trying to steal the hawksbill. Who are you people with? Aren't you from U.S. Fish and Wildlife?"

"No, sir. We're immigration officials," the man answered. Turning to two of the uniformed officers—one of them a woman—who'd come ashore with him, he said, "Take these smugglers onto the boat and secure them while we search for the cargo before they get too far away. Radio the other unit to cover everything in the area of the 3-mile marker on North Shore Road. We'll have to move fast before the aliens escape."

"Aliens?" Ashley cried. "You mean like aliens from outer space?"

The officer gave a short bark of laughter. "No, honey. Illegal aliens. From Haiti. These two men have been smuggling illegal aliens to St. John for quite a while now. Didn't you see all those people running to shore? They weren't here for the turtle. No, this is the first stop for a lot of illegals on their route to the U.S. mainland."

Moving silently, Forrest had crept up behind Jack. He tugged on Jack's arm as though he hadn't attacked him just moments before. "Please," he whispered, "Jack, please, I have to talk to you."

Jack pulled away because he knew what Forrest was going to say. Both of them had seen Cimmaron there in the trees. Jack was the only one of the Landons who'd seen her help the illegals escape. Clearly Cimmaron was part of a team that not only smuggled turtles, but smuggled humans as well. It was his duty to report her to the immigration officers.

"Jack!" Forrest was pleading now. "Please let me just say what I have to say. I'm...I'm sorry about what I did back there, but there's a reason. Let me at least tell you."

"Forget it," Jack growled. Forrest might be a smooth talker, but it wouldn't make any difference. Right was right, honest was honest, legal was legal. Besides, his arms were beginning to throb from where Forrest had pounded them into the ground. No way did he feel like talking to Forrest.

"Just hear me out. If you don't change your mind, I'll do whatever you say. Come on, Jack."

He looked so desperate that Jack found himself saying, "OK. Make it quick!"

As the two of them moved to the rocky part of the beach, they noticed that the female hawksbill had somehow found her way back to shore. She began once again to cover her nest with sand, trying desperately to finish the job she'd come to do. Jack glanced behind him. His parents were busy answering the questions of a female immigration officer while Ashley watched, wide-eyed, taking in every word. No one realized that Jack and Forrest had left the rest of the group.

"OK," Jack demanded, turning his anger full force onto Forrest. "Say what you're going to say. It won't change a thing."

"I know you saw Cimmaron, but no one else did."

"So?"

"That means unless they catch her tonight, no one will be able to prove she's part of the smuggling operation. The men she was working with have already been arrested, so they won't be doing any more smuggling or poaching. I want you to let Cimmaron go." Forrest was shivering, even though the night felt warm.

"You want me to ignore the fact that Cimmaron is a smuggler."

"Yes."

"What if those immigration officers start asking me questions?"

"Lie."

"I can't." Jack shook his head decisively. "Not anymore. I kept your secret and look what happened. It almost got a hawksbill killed—"

"Cimmaron didn't know anything about the turtle poaching."

"You don't know that!" Jack punched Forrest's chest with his fist and declared, "You don't know anything, Forrest. No, I'm through lying for you. Cimmaron's on her own. And so are you."

Forrest put his hands over his eyes and pulled his fingers slowly down his face so hard that it distorted his features. Jack almost felt sorry for him. Almost.

"OK," Forrest said at last. "Will you at least keep your distance from the immigration officers? Don't volunteer anything. Don't say anything to your parents."

"I have to do what's right—"

"Look, I'm asking you, Jack. No, I'm begging you! Please don't tell." In a broken voice, Forrest said, "She's my mother."

CHAPTER TWELVE

The room was about a hundred times nicer than the ones the Landons were staying in. It was a suite of rooms, actually, in the finest hotel on St. John. Large French windows offered a full view of Cruz Bay, dotted as always with the white sails of yachts. In a corner next to the windows stood a palm tree, small but real, its fronds swaying slightly in the breeze from the air conditioner. In the center of the room, a low table held pitchers of fruit juice, a bowl of tropical fruit, and a plate of delicate pastries.

Six cushioned chairs formed a semicircle, all of them facing a tapestried sofa where two people sat. The man, who had thinning gray hair, wore a dress shirt, open at the neck, and pleated tan slacks. The woman was dressed more elegantly and wore several gold bracelets on each arm.

Forrest had been surprised, to put it mildly, when he entered the suite with the Landons and found his father sitting there along with his mother. "I thought this was important enough that I should come," Forrest Winthrop III told Forrest Winthrop IV, even before he said hello. "I had to rearrange some meetings, but here I am, son."

Mrs. Winthrop had hugged Forrest and kissed his cheek. Although Mr. Winthrop seemed a lot older than Jack had expected—his face was lined and his shoulders stooped a bit—Mrs. Winthrop looked a lot younger than she probably was. Her blond hair hung in a sweep that ended just below her chin, the skin on her face stretched taut over high cheekbones, and her brows were perfectly shaped. Jack had never before seen a woman quite as elegant as Mrs. Winthrop.

During the silence that hung in the room after all of them were seated, Mr. Winthrop took a cigar from a silver case. With some sort of tool, he cut the end from the cigar, then lit it with a flame that shot up from a matching silver lighter, rotating the unlit end of the cigar around and around in his lips as he puffed until it was smoldering satisfactorily. Jack watched the procedure, rather fascinated by the whole thing. Only after it was finished did Mr. Winthrop glance up and say, "You're looking well, Cimmaron."

Cimmaron's chair stood directly across from the Winthrops. If she was about to face a grilling, she was in the right position for it. "Both of you are looking good also," she answered. "Mrs. Winthrop, you haven't changed one bit in 13 years."

Smiling slightly, Mrs. Winthrop brushed her own cheek delicately with the tip of her manicured fingers. "I have to work at it, Cimmaron," she said, with a trace of humor directed at herself.

"So let's get down to business," Mr. Winthrop said. "I believe I have been filled in on all the particulars by Mr. and Mrs.—uh, Landon." He hesitated over the name as though he weren't too sure of it.

"Dr. Landon," Olivia said sweetly. "I'm Dr. Landon."

Jack and Ashley exchanged surprised glances. Their mother never pulled rank like that.

"So!" Mr. Winthrop continued, "In the interest of saving time, I'm going to ask you point-blank, Cimmaron. Are you in the business of smuggling illegal aliens?"

"No," she answered abruptly.

"Hmm." Mr. Winthrop tapped ashes from his cigar into a round ashtray on a stand next to the sofa. "My acquaintance in the immigration division informed me that last night a boatload of illegal aliens landed at Jumbie Bay. Were you in any way involved in that operation, Cimmaron?"

"Yes," she answered. "I was at Jumbie Bay last night."

Jack let out such a big sigh that his father turned to stare at him. What a relief! In all the hours since Forrest had begged him not to squeal on Cimmaron, Jack had wrestled with his conscience, wondering what to do. To tell, or not to tell? And now he no longer had to make a decision, because Cimmaron herself had just admitted to being there last night. Through narrowed eyes, Forrest gave a slight nod to Jack that must have meant "you're off the hook."

"You say you are not in the business of smuggling illegal aliens," Mr. Winthrop continued, pointing the cigar at Cimmaron, "and yet you admit that you were involved in what happened last night."

"What about the turtles?" Olivia asked.

"Turtles!" Cimmaron exclaimed almost scornfully. "I have nothing to do with turtles." Her gaze intense, she leaned forward in her chair. "My only care is for the people—as your Statue of Liberty says, 'the wretched refuse.' Never have I ever taken a single penny for helping the illegals."

"Well, those men who got arrested last night—Arlen Smith and Bené Phillipe—were making a pretty profit," Mr. Winthrop told her. "They charge the Haitians thousands of dollars to smuggle them here."

"If the Haitians arrive because smugglers bring them, that is not any of my affair," Cimmaron declared. "All I try to do is help them when they reach St. John."

"Do you take these people into your home?" Mr. Winthrop asked.

"I do what is needed. Sometimes I shelter them, more often I bring them to a very special person who lives high in the hills, in a remote area where the immigration officials never think to look. She hides them and feeds them and teaches them how to stay alive on St. John."

Miss Amelia! Jack was sure it had to be Miss Amelia, with her ramshackle house perched on the top of a hill, with her knowledge of herbs and medicines and her experience of life lived by passing through hardship. He could tell that Ashley made the same connection—she grinned at Jack, then silently mouthed the word "Miss," but he shook his head before she got to "Amelia." Did Denise know about this? Jack wondered. No, Denise wouldn't want to know, even if she suspected. Denise was an employee of the U.S. government. If she became aware that Miss Amelia was sheltering illegal immigrants, she'd have to report it.

"So you transport these illegals around the island, Cimmaron?" Mr. Winthrop persisted.

"Yes."

"Hand me my briefcase, dear," Mr. Winthrop told his wife. When she did, he snapped open the clasps and took out several papers. After slipping on a pair of eyeglasses that rested near the bottom of his nose, he began to read, "A person commits a federal felony when he or she assists an alien by transporting, sheltering, or helping him to obtain employment. Any vehicle used to transport illegal aliens may be seized by an immigration officer and is subject to forfeiture."

At that, Forrest burst out laughing. "You mean the Feds are going to take away Cimmaron's car? You should see the car, Dad. It's held together with duct tape and paper clips."

"This is hardly the time for levity, son. This is very serious business."

For the first time, Mrs. Winthrop spoke up. "Cimmaron, dear, why do you involve yourself with illegal aliens? You say you're not being paid to do it, and you might end up in jail."

Cimmaron answered in a voice that started out calm, but rose in volume as she went on. "I'm a poor black woman from St. John, but compared to the people of Haiti, I live like a queen. Daily life in Haiti is a terrible struggle. Three-quarters of the people have no jobs. No income. Less than half the children go to school. Life expectancy is age 45. Political violence—"

"But that's none of your concern, is it?" Mrs. Winthrop interrupted.

Now Cimmaron's dark eyes began to blaze. "Not my concern! These people live in the worst kind of poverty and in constant fear that they won't be able to feed their children. I help them because I know what it feels like. I was there! I was one of them. To escape from fear, I too had to sign a paper that I would somehow pay the smugglers thousands of dollars. And when I was slow paying, they threatened my child. Why do you think I let you adopt Forrest?"

Forrest half rose from his chair, then sank back into it.

Raising her head defiantly, Cimmaron continued, "I wanted my baby to have a decent chance, and now I'm helping desperate Haitians find their own decent chance. Here on St. John they work hard and live on next to nothing so they can send money home to their families. If they're very lucky, the United States government might let them apply for a green card, and then they can become legal."

Mr. Winthrop murmured, "Section 245(i) of the Legal Immigration Family Equity Act has expired. And since the terrorist attacks in 2001, security is much tighter at all points of entry. Many more illegals are getting caught and turned back."

This time Forrest stood all the way up. "Wait a minute, Dad. Businesses still hire illegal workers, and the Immigration Service looks the other way. You know why? Because factories and service companies need people who will work at cheap jobs that American citizens don't want. If all the illegals in the U.S. were deported, it would cripple American business and hurt growth. Our whole economy would collapse. So...!" He raised a finger to emphasize his point. "If factory owners aren't punished for hiring illegals, why should Cimmaron be punished for helping poor people find food and shelter?"

His eyes narrowing, Mr. Winthrop asked, "Where did you hear all that?"

"In economics class," Forrest answered.

Economics! Forrest was the same age as Jack, and he was studying economics? What kind of school did he go to? In Jack's junior high, the most advanced class for eighth graders was pre-algebra.

Mr. Winthrop frowned as he stated, "Much of what you've said is an exaggeration, Forrest, although there's...some truth to it."

"And so?" Forrest asked expectantly.

Turning to Cimmaron, Mr. Winthrop answered, "And so...this one time, I'll help you escape the consequences of your actions, as long as you promise me that you won't be involved again with any illegal immigrants."

"And if I don't promise?" Cimmaron asked softly.

"Then you may...possibly...face jail time."

Striding toward his father, Forrest stated, "If they put her in jail, then I'll be here to help the illegals. I want to come and live with Cimmaron. She needs me."

A small cry escaped Mrs. Winthrop, who looked stricken. Mr. Winthrop, however, stated flatly, "You can forget that, Forrest. You're our son. I gave you my name. Three generations of Winthrops have been called Forrest, and you are the fourth."

"Yes, but before that, I had another name," Forrest declared. "Cimmaron told me what she named me when I was born. Aquashi, for the prince of the Aquambo tribe. I am his descendant."

To Jack, it no longer seemed that he was in a theater watching a drama—he now felt like the worst kind of intruder, hearing raw emotion he had no right to hear. Ashley, sitting next to him, had begun to choke up with tears. Olivia clutched the arms of her chair while Steven looked at the floor, his jaw working. Only Forrest seemed in full command of himself.

"I cannot accept that," Mr. Winthrop said. "You are my son, Forrest, and you will stay with me."

"Then," Forrest told his father, "you and I will have to negotiate. I will attend all the prominent prep schools and universities you choose to send me to, but I will spend my summers here on St. John. With Cimmaron."

When Mr. Winthrop rose to answer his son, Jack was struck by how alike they seemed. Forrest might be the son of Cimmaron and a young American idealist, but his mannerisms were exact copies of his adoptive father's. They stood with the same self-assurance, holding the same pose—chins high, eyes locked on each other's, rocking forward slightly on their toes.

"Two weeks," Mr. Winthrop declared. "Two weeks each summer you may come to St. John. That is, if that is agreeable with you," he said, with a slight, formal nod toward Cimmaron

"No, it is not." Cimmaron hesitated, then murmured, "I would prefer…."

Jack held his breath. If Cimmaron was about to say that she would prefer never to see Forrest again, Forrest would be devastated, and the whole thing would be too painful for Jack to watch. He wanted to run away, the way he used to run into his bedroom to hide in the middle of a scary movie on TV. But there was no place to go. Besides, he couldn't leave now. Every eye in the room was focused on Cimmaron.

"I would prefer," she said, "that he come for *three* weeks each summer. I also prefer that he work hard at school, so that he will be able to fight in the courts to change the immigration laws. You said you could help me, Forrest. That is how you could do the most good."

"I'll do that, Cimmaron," Forrest told her. "I promise."

"As for me," Cimmaron said, "here's my promise. I will no longer help any illegal immigrants smuggled into St. John by Arlen Smith and Bené Phillipe.*"

At that Ashley stifled a little giggle, and everyone else had to smile. Arlen Smith and Bené Phillipe had been arrested at Jumbie Bay the night before. Since they'd be going to prison for a long time, they wouldn't be smuggling any more illegal immigrants into St. John.

The tension was broken. Mrs. Winthrop rushed to Forrest to tell him how much he meant to her, how she'd loved him from the moment she first saw him. Mr. Winthrop stood there smiling slightly, a little glint in his eye, perhaps secretly proud that his son had pulled this off. Forrest had attitude, as well as smarts, a combination that spelled success.

At a signal from Steven, the four Landons quietly slipped out of the room, leaving Forrest with his two mothers and his father, the diplomat.

Jack laughed when Ashley came up sputtering—as much as he could laugh with the mouthpiece of a snorkel between his teeth. Spitting it out, he told her, "Don't stand on the coral! Tread water. Swim over here, and I'll tighten the strap on your mask so you won't get such a snoot full."

"Ow! Ow!" she cried as a few strands of her hair got caught in the strap Jack was adjusting. "You're doing that on purpose."

"No I'm not. That ought to work now. Did you see the underwater markers?"

Alone at last, Steven, Olivia, Jack, and Ashley were exploring the underwater park, where a dozen varieties of coral and other reef creatures had been identified by plaques sunk into the bottom of Trunk Bay. Red, white, and blue buoys marked the route of the underwater trail. With Ashley paddling right after him, Jack followed the trail, pointing down to draw Ashley's attention to the staghorn and elkhorn coral, the sea fans, and the tiny, delicate, purple anemones.

Since Ashley was swimming behind Jack, whenever she wanted to show him something, she would grab one of his feet and pull it. He didn't mind, because he didn't want to miss anything. Dangling from a cord around his neck was an underwater camera he'd rented. As each species came into view through the clear, turquoise water, he would take careful aim and shoot, being cautious not to waste his shots, because it would be too difficult to change film that far from shore.

They drifted through swarms of blue needle-nosed fish thinner than pencils and were surrounded by hordes of tiny fish as thick as gnats, so plentiful that they should have been bumping into one another and Jack, but they never did. "Awesome," he thought.

Turning himself around, Jack peered into the coral reef that rose up in castle-like spires. It was then he saw it—the dark, mottled-brown shape gliding across the coral tips, bobbing up to the surface for a quick gulp of air before sailing down to the reef once again. A hawksbill!

In an instant Jack reared up, yanking his mask off in order to call his family. When he told them what he'd found, an expression of sheer delight lit up his mother's face. "You know, it might be the female we saved last night—wouldn't that be incredible! Where is she?"

"Follow me!" Jack commanded, securing his mask. As he placed his face down into the water, once again he had the feeling he had entered a giant aquarium, one with colors created from a palette not found on dry land. A fish painted in orange and black stripes shot past, while one as bright as a lemon darted only three feet beyond Jack's hand. But where was the turtle? For a moment he thought the hawksbill had vanished, until he finally caught sight of her paddling blissfully to the surface, as graceful in the water as a dolphin.

The other three Landons gave Jack a "thumbs up," smiling as much as they could with snorkels wedged in their mouths. Jack felt his throat tighten with emotion. The reality of what had nearly happened hit him full-face: This beautiful, gentle creature had almost died at the hands of men who cared only for money. Although the poachers had been caught, Jack knew there were more of them out there, waiting. The coral reef was dying, too, its fragile perfection smothered by runoff soil as land was cleared for buildings. Other parts of the reef had been shattered by boat anchors. But at least there would be no more anchor damage in Jumbie Bay, now that those smugglers had been caught.

When he felt a tug on his swim fin, Jack raised his head above water and stared right into Ashley's face.

"What's up?" Ashley asked, treading water like a puppy. Leave it to his sister to read his face, even behind a mask.

"Nothing."

"Come on, Jack. What?"

"I guess...I guess I was thinking that the hawksbills are still not safe. What if poachers keep killing them? They'll become extinct, gone forever! And the reef—oh, I don't know."

"It won't happen, not if people fight it. Forrest is going to law school to protect the Haitians. Why don't you go, too? Then you can protect the turtles and the coral reefs." She was beginning to pant, because it was harder to float while treading water than when stretched out, facedown. Jack felt his own heart beat faster as he worked his arms and legs.

"You mean you want me to be a lawyer?"

"Maybe. Or maybe not. Just so you do *something* to save the Earth!" Ashley gave him a playful splash and pushed the end of the snorkel back into her mouth. With a swish of her fins she was gone, joining Steven and Olivia as they hovered over the place where the turtle had been.

A wave buoyed Jack up and down, rocking him as gently as a baby in a cradle. He felt the soft breeze on his cheeks, working with the sun to dry his skin until it felt taut with salt. Ashley was right. His life stretched ahead of him as far as the ocean. Anything was possible. Forrest had come to this small island to find someone who mattered to him. Well, Jack had found something, as well. There was work to do. Work *he* could do.

The rhythm of the ocean carried him forward and back, an eternal tide of beginnings and endings.

AFTERWORD

Beneath the surface of the clear, tropical waters of Virgin Islands National Park lie the beautiful coral reefs that captivated Ashley and Jack. A never-ending parade of activity and color, coral reefs are central to the lives of millions of species of animals and plants. While some creatures are full-time residents, some are visitors just passing through. Others are underwater commuters, traveling daily from nearby habitats (the "suburbs") to the coral "cities." Rush-hour traffic peaks at dawn and dusk. At dusk, reef fish, such as grunts and snappers, and invertebrate carnivores, such as lobsters, race away from the reef to dine in the nearby seagrass and algal plains communities. Traveling in the opposite direction, parrotfish return to the coral city and join the many other fish and invertebrate species seeking shelter in the reef at night. At dawn, the scene reverses.

Some creatures have a *much* longer commute. Every few years the female Hawksbill sea turtle, encased in her beautiful shell, travels from the coral reefs where she feeds on sponges and zoanthids (sea anemone-like animals), across one thousand miles of open ocean to the beach where she hatched from an egg. She crawls from the sea onto the beach where she began life and uses her flippers to dig a pit in the sand. There she lays her eggs, covers them with sand, and returns to the sea—to begin her long trip back to the reefs where she feeds.

As you can see, coral reefs do not exist in isolation. Their health is deeply connected to the quality of the water and the health of nearby and distant communities of tropical marine habitats, such as the seagrass beds and algal plains.

Coral reefs have survived millions of years of Mother Nature's tests: hurricanes, winter storms, diseases, warmer water, colder water, higher sea levels, lower sea levels, predators. As if Mother Nature's tests were not enough, humankind's destructive activities add further stress to coral reefs. Boats run aground, anchors are improperly placed, and careless snorkelers and divers stand on the coral. Soil runs off cleared land and smothers near-shore reefs. Sewage, oil spills, and other pollutants, such as fertilizers and pesticides, can degrade water quality to the point that coral reef organisms can no longer live. Heavy fishing pressure reduces the numbers and sizes of fish and removes most of the large predators, which eventually changes the way the reef functions.

Today, coral reefs worldwide are in decline. Although we cannot stop coral-eating predators, hurricanes, or winter storms, we can help coral reefs survive. We can minimize our destructive or careless activities, and we can use the best scientific information to design ways to help reefs recover from damage. At Virgin Islands National Park, we have tried to do both. Scientists, community volunteers, and students of the 5th-6th grade science class from a local school worked together on a coral transplant project that combined community education and scientific research on coral reefs. The purpose of the project was to find a simple, easy, non-destructive way to transplant living coral to damaged reefs in an attempt to speed the reef's recovery.

The first problem was where to find the corals to transplant. Mother Nature provided the answer. Many species of coral reproduce by fragmentation. Pieces of coral are broken off large coral colonies by the force of large waves produced by winter storms or hurricanes. The fragments of coral roll around on the bottom until they either lodge firmly in a crack in the reef or are scoured by sand and sediment and die. By collecting coral fragments from sandy areas where they had little chance of surviving, the research team had a ready source of corals to transplant and the fragments had an increased chance of survival. Plastic cable ties proved to be the most inexpensive, easy, effective way to attach the pieces of coral to the transplant reef. Every month, the team snorkeled out to the reef, photographed the colonies, and recorded observations on the condition of the transplanted corals and on an equal number of the reef's naturally occurring colonies. When the two-year study ended, we found that the survival of the transplanted corals was nearly the same as corals found naturally on the reef. Success! Transplanting had not harmed the coral fragments. In fact, most of them probably were saved from being buried or worn down by sand. Although a damaged reef can never be restored to its original state, this method may be used on a larger scale in the future to help coral reefs recover.

We have a long way to go before we completely understand the workings of coral reefs and the tropical underwater world. If Jack does choose to study the beautiful and complex world of coral reefs, he will find a wealth of exciting questions to be answered and problems to be solved.

Ginger Garrison
Marine Ecologist
U.S. Geological Survey

DON'T MISS—

WOLF STALKER
MYSTERY #1
Fast-paced adventure has the Landons on the trail
of a wounded wolf in Yellowstone National Park.

CLIFF-HANGER
MYSTERY #2
Jack's desire to help the headstrong Lucky Deal
brings him face-to-face with a hungry cougar in
Mesa Verde National Park.

DEADLY WATERS
MYSTERY #3
Jack and Ashley's efforts to save an injured manatee
involve them in a thrilling chase through the Everglades.

RAGE OF FIRE
MYSTERY #4
In this tale of myth and mystery, a Vietnamese orphan
named Danny leads Ashley and Jack into a steaming
crater in Hawaii Volcanoes National Park.

THE HUNTED
MYSTERY #5
While attempting to help a young Mexican runaway, Jack
and Ashley flee for their lives from an enraged mother
grizzly in Glacier National Park.

GHOST HORSES
MYSTERY #6
Life-threatening accidents plague the Landons as they
investigate the mysterious deaths of some white mustangs
on a trip to Zion National Park.

OVER THE EDGE
MYSTERY #7
Jack relies on high-tech cyber skills to find out who is
threatening his mother after she broadcasts her plan to
save the condors in Grand Canyon National Park.

VALLEY OF DEATH
MYSTERY #8
A showdown with Ashley's kidnappers leads the Landons
to a missile testing ground and the key to what's killing the
desert bighorn sheep in Death Valley National Park.

COMING SOON—

OUT OF THE DEEP
MYSTERY #10

*To read samples from each of these mysteries,
go to Gloria Skurzynski's Web site:*
http://gloriabooks.com/national.html

ABOUT THE AUTHORS

An award-winning mystery writer and an award-winning science writer—who are also mother and daughter—are working together on Mysteries in Our National Parks!

Alane (Lanie) Ferguson's first mystery, *Show Me the Evidence,* won the Edgar Award, given by the Mystery Writers of America.

Gloria Skurzynski's *Almost the Real Thing* won the American Institute of Physics Science Writing Award.

Lanie lives in Elizabeth, Colorado. Gloria lives in Boise, Idaho. To work together on a novel, they connect by phone, fax, and e-mail and "often forget which one of us wrote a particular line."

Gloria's e-mail: gloriabooks@qwest.net
Her Web site: http://gloriabooks.com
Lanie's e-mail: aferguson@sprynet.com
Her Web site: http://alaneferguson.com

One of the world's largest nonprofit scientific and educational organizations, the National Geographic Society was founded in 1888 "for the increase and diffusion of geographic knowledge." Fulfilling this mission, the Society educates and inspires millions every day through its magazines, books, television programs, videos, maps and atlases, research grants, the National Geographic Bee, teacher workshops, and innovative classroom materials. The Society is supported through membership dues, charitable gifts, and income from the sale of its educational products. This support is vital to National Geographic's mission to increase global understanding and promote conservation of our planet through exploration, research, and education. For more information, please call 1-800-NGS LINE (647-5463) or write to the following address:

NATIONAL GEOGRAPHIC SOCIETY
1145 17th Street N.W.
Washington, D.C. 20036-4688
U.S.A.
Visit the Society's Web site: www.nationalgeographic.com